DREAM ON

About the Authors

Steve Skidmore lives in Leicester, Steve Barlow has recently moved to rural Somerset. Since meeting in Nottingham fifteen years ago, they have been working as a duo both as performing artists and as writers. To date they have written eighty books together.

Their performances have been described as 'hilarious', 'entertaining', 'brilliant' and 'mad'. The Two Steves have also written a unique series combining books and the internet, OUTERNET.

Their series MAD MYTHS, published by Barn Owl, have proved very popular.

For Lauren

STEVE BARLOW & STEVE SKIDMORE

DREAM ON

BARN OWL BOOKS

BARN OWL BOOKS

157 Fortis Green Road, London, N10 3LX

First published by Piccadilly Press, London, 1998

This edition published by Barn Owl Books, 2009
157 Fortis Green Road, London, N10 3LX

Distributed by Frances Lincoln
4 Torriano Mews, Torriano Avenue, London, NW5 2RZ

Text copyright © Steve Barlow & Steve Skidmore, 1998, 2009

ISBN 978 19 0 301579 7

Designed and set by Skandesign Limited
Produced in Poland by Polskabook

www.barnowlbooks.com

Quotations from the 1939 Collins edition of *Romeo and Juliet*.

"...I talk of dreams;
Which are the children of an idle brain,
Begot of nothing but vain fantasy..."

William Shakespeare
(Romeo and Juliet, I. iv)

PROLOGUE

Two lovers, both alike in vanity,
      Far from Verona act their sorry scene.
For Charlie's love is sheer insanity;
      Alas, poor girl, what can she do but dream?
From forth the fateful story of their woes,
      This tale of school-cursed lovers ends in strife;
Whose misadventures, shamelessly disclosed,
      May make the reader wish she'd get a life.
This tale of Charlie's unrequited love,
      (So full of passion, pain, romance and rage)
Is told in words that all to tears will move
      As hope and heartache drip from every page.
If you have tears, prepare to shed them, friend;
      Your hankie will be soaked before the end.

ACT 1

ACT 1, SCENE 1

Hear the sentence of your movéd prince.
(Romeo and Juliet, 1.i)

The hot sun kissed her tanned body as she lay on the golden sands of her own private tropical island paradise. The island had cost a fortune, but she was the world's greatest movie star. She HAD a fortune. In fact, she had several.

Garth Strong, Hollywood's second-hottest movie star, scowled at her. When Garth narrowed his eyes, women in cinemas all over the world fainted. He narrowed them now.

"Goddamit, Charlie," he snarled, "you GOTTA do this movie!"

Did Garth really think she was going to fall for the he-man routine? She ignored him. His shoulders slumped. He knelt brokenly in the sand beside her.

"Charlie," he murmured huskily, "I guess we're all counting on you. The picture needs you. The director needs you..."

"Gee, I don't know, Garth." She took another sip of iced champagne. "I kinda promised Stevie Spielberg..."

Tears came to Garth's steel blue eyes. "Charlie," he whispered, " I need you..."

His pleading hand reached for her cheek. Their eyes locked in a timeless moment. Sounds faded: the sigh of the wind, the crash of the surf, the cries of...

"Charlotte Robbins, stop daydreaming!"

I sat bolt upright, looked around in panic as the rest of the class burst into raucous laughter.

"And the rest of you rabble can stop that noise!"

shouted Mr Brooks. "This is supposed to be a maths lesson, not feeding time at a chimps' tea party".

The class immediately clammed up; Mr Brooks was Not a Teacher To Be Messed With. He stared around the room to make sure that all sniggers had ceased before turning back to me and resuming his attack. "Well, Charlotte, a new school year, a new exam class and the same old head-in-the-clouds you. Perhaps you'd like to tell me what I've been standing here saying?"

"A new school year, a new exam class and the sa..."

"Before that!" he snapped.

A hot, embarrassed flush sprang across my cheeks as I felt the rest of the class trying to suppress a laugh.

"Er... something to do with maths...?" I whined hopefully. The flush was travelling rapidly down my backbone towards my knees via my bottom.

"Incredible! This is a maths lesson, I'm a maths teacher and maybe, just maybe, I've been talking about maths! Miss Robbins, with such deductive powers, I am amazed that Scotland Yard aren't banging on your door, pleading with you to put your mind-numbingly brilliant logic towards their files of unsolved crimes." Mr Brooks was the World Champion in Sarcasm and Nastiness. "Well, I'm going to tell you what I was talking about whilst you were daydreaming..."

"Thank you Sir," I muttered, relieved to get off so lightly.

"...tomorrow lunch-time."

I sat crestfallen. Detention! On the first day of term! Just my luck. I turned towards Amy who grinned supportively and shrugged her shoulders.

"Never mind," she whispered. "Everyone knows he's

a dodo."

The 'dodo' continued. "So, for the benefit of Charlotte, if Y is a prime number and the two sides of the triangle are equal, what does X equal?"

"Who gives a monkeys?" I thought as I stared blankly at the meaningless squiggles on the whiteboard.

"And the winner of this year's Nobel Prize for Mathematics, is Professor Charlie Robbins, for her work in proving that Isaac Newton, Albert Einstein and Stephen Hawking were totally wrong about everything to do with mathematics and that the universe is actually made up of rotting cheese."

Charlie smiled. All around her the Nobel delegates stood applauding wildly as she made her way to the rostrum to collect the cheque for a million dollars. It had taken years of research, but her hunch had finally paid off. Her name would go down in history as the greatest mathematical mind ever. This would show Mr Dodo Brooks thought Charlie as she climbed the red carpeted stairs. He believed I couldn't do maths and now, here I am receiving the acclaim of the greatest minds in the world for having proved that all matter is made up of...

"So what is the answer, Charlotte?"

"...rotting cheese."

There was a collective "Huh?" from the rest of the class. I sat gaping with horror as my brain caught up with my mouth and I realised what I'd said. The roar from Mr Brooks hit me like a tornado. "Make that a double detention!"

ACT 1, SCENE 2

Tell me in sadness, who is it that you love?
(Romeo and Juliet,I.i)

"That's got to be a world record," said Amy as we sat in our form room at lunch-time. "A double detention in the first maths lesson on the first day of the new school year."

"You sound just like Brooks," I snapped. "It wasn't fair. I couldn't help drifting off. I was bored."

"Of course you were. We all were," Amy said matter-of-factly. "That's what maths is for. To bore people so much, that all the other lessons you have to do seem all right. You've got to do what I'm going to do; grit my teeth, get through two years of boring figures and equations, pass the exam and never look at another maths book for the rest of my life."

"Hmm, suppose so," I agreed. Amy's logic was, as usual, spot on.

"So, what were you daydreaming about this time?" she asked.

"Doesn't matter. Anyway, you wouldn't believe it..." I didn't fancy telling her about winning the Nobel Prize. She'd think I was going gaga. And I certainly wasn't going to let on about the Garth daydream...

"Come on, tell me."

I was rescued by the form room door crashing open. A sports bag shot across the room. Tom Davies followed it in.

"Hiya!"

Amy and I chorused a hiya back. Tom picked up his bag and plonked himself on the table next to us. "Heard

13

about the rotting cheese! Well done, Charlie; must be a detention world record, even for Brooks!"

"All right," I replied wearily, "don't go on."

"OK, OK. Did you have a good holiday?" Tom was good at changing the subject when he needed to.

"Oh, not bad," I said, airily. "I won Wimbledon, recorded a hit single that stayed at Number One all summer, discovered a cure for all known diseases, repaired the hole in the ozone layer and got elected pope."

"Really?"

I looked heavenwards. "No. I had two weeks of family holiday hell on a Dorset campsite, then four weeks of nothing."

Hell was the right word for fourteen days of constant rain and constant squabbling with my family, followed by four weeks of having to look after Nick (my brat of a younger brother) because Mum was away on an Open University course, and Dad was working at the counselling centre.

"Surely you did something!" Tom queried. "Didn't you go round Amy's or something...?"

I glared at Amy. "No. She was away *all* summer."

Amy shrugged. "I couldn't help it if my mum and dad wanted to play I'm-going-to-give-our-daughter-a-better-holiday-than-you-to-prove-I'm-a-better-parent-than-you-are competition." She smiled at Tom. "I had three weeks in Florida with Mum and her boyfriend and then three weeks in France and Spain with Dad and his girlfriend."

"Lucky you," whistled Tom. "Which parent won?"

Amy grinned. "I told Dad that Mum's holiday was the best and I told Mum that it was Dad's. So next year they'll both try even harder and I'll get two fantastic holidays again. Oh yeah, and they're also fighting about who can take me skiing at Christmas!"

I shook my head. Unbelievable! Still, I couldn't be too jealous of Amy. She'd been through a rotten time when her Mum and Dad split up. It was amazing how she handled it all. Nevertheless, I still launched into my well-rehearsed self-pitying speech. "You know those essays we had to write without fail at infant school and junior school at the beginning of every new school year: 'What I did on my holidays'?"

Amy and Tom nodded.

"Well, this year I could finish that in two words: 'I didn't'."

"Oh come on Charlie," Tom protested. "You must have done *something*."

"Okay, if you don't believe me, look at my diary." I reached into my bag and pulled out my Filofax diary that Mum and Dad had bought me for my birthday. That's how much they know about me, I thought - I could write the exciting and significant moments in my life on the back of a postage stamp and still have space for the complete works of Shakespeare.

Charlie opened her designer-made, red leather-bound diary and turned the thick, luxurious pages. She glanced down the page and shook her head. She spoke softly into the phone. "I'm sorry Garth, but I just can't make it this week."

"But why not, Charlie? Why not?" She could hear the quiver in Garth's voice.

She ran her fingers down the page "Well, I'm guest of honour at the Monte Carlo Grand Prix on Sunday, I have the Madrid, London AND Paris fashion shows on Monday; Tuesday, I have to open a new orphanage for children with leprosy in India;

on Wednesday I've promised the United Nations that I'll speak on World Poverty in New York, Thursday I have an all-day sitting for a new portrait for the National Gallery, Friday I have a state banquet at Buckingham Palace and Saturday I'm washing my hair. I'm sorry, it's just not possible."

"But Charlie, please..." She could hear his voice breaking up. "I've got to see you. I can't live without you. Without you life is just a meaningless nothing," sobbed Garth.

"Well, if it'll make you feel a bit better, I suppose I could see you for just a few minutes before the state banquet."

"Yes, oh thank you, thank you, thank you."

"Poor lost puppy," murmured Charlie as she replaced the receiver.

"Pass it over then," Tom put out his hand. "Let's see what you're moaning about."

I opened the Filofax and showed him a typical fun-filled, action packed week of my holidays.

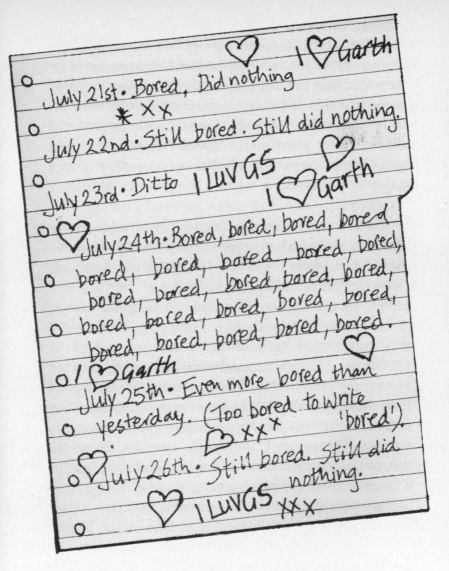

July 21st · Bored, Did nothing
I ♡ Garth
♡ ✳ XX

July 22nd · Still bored. Still did nothing.

July 23rd · Ditto I LUV GS ♡
I ♡ Garth

♡ July 24th · Bored, bored.

I ♡ Garth ♡

July 25th · Even more bored than yesterday. (Too bored to write 'bored').
♡ XXX

July 26th · Still bored. Still did nothing.
♡ ♡ I LUV GS XXX

Instead of offering any words of comfort, Tom immediately burst out laughing. "I heart Garth!" he hooted, "I luv GS!"

I snatched the diary back. "Not that bit..."

"Ooh, touchy..." laughed Tom, "... and embarrassing!"

He held his hands up towards my face and pretended to warm them as I felt a hot flush spreading across my cheeks for the second time that day. The dreaded red flush - aaghhhh! At the first sign of any embarrassing situation, I become an instant walking tomato. I'd had to cope with the affliction ever since infant school. My nickname had been 'Robin Redbreast' which I was awarded after a major embarrassment when I forgot my lines in a nativity play.

The teacher who was directing the play, one Mrs Hardy (the cow), made the link between my name, Christmas and the fact that I went bright red. "Charlotte aren't you just like a little robin redbreast?" Ho, ho, ho, aren't teachers funny? Of course like all nicknames that you hate, it stuck. Thanks very much Mrs Hardy (cow, first-class). I was condemned to years of taunts, (especially at Christmas). These increased dramatically when I started to wear my very first bra. The boys in my class had a great time amusing their pre-pubescent sense of humour. Even nowadays a few spotty, testosterone-filled nerds occasionally resurrect the *double entendre* to amuse themselves and show off to their mates. And all because of a throwaway remark by a teacher (*cow, cow, cow!*).

By now, my flush was turning from light pink to a deep crimson as Amy shook her head "Not STILL Garth? Honestly Charlie. Garth Strong!" she sighed.

Yup. 'Fraid so. Still Garth Strong. I'd fancied him for ages. Flowing hair, blue eyes, rippling muscles. Some of the girls thought he was well fit, but they were stupid. He was drop-dead gorgeous.

"Why shouldn't I?" I snapped back. "Why should I be different? Every girl in the school thinks he's sex on legs."

Tom sniggered. Amy nodded solemnly. "If you say so."

"Well, they do."

"I don't," said Amy.

Although I was inwardly pleased to hear that my best friend didn't fancy the love of my life, I nevertheless sprang to Garth's defence. "What's wrong with him?" I demanded.

"I suppose I don't fancy blokes who spend more time in front of a mirror than me," Amy replied cattily.

I gave her a death stare. She returned it.

"Amy's right, Charlie," Tom piped up. "I can't believe you've got the hots for Garth Why-Shouldn't-I-Fancy-Me-Everyone-Else-Does Strong. Everyone knows he's a poser."

"He can't help being good looking."

"Good-looking?!!" Tom nearly choked. "You need more than glasses. You need a guide dog!"

"Just stop going on about Garth." I snapped. "You were supposed to be looking at what I did, or rather, didn't do, during the holidays."

I handed Tom back the diary. He glanced down the page again. "Were you bored then?"

My reply was drowned out by the bell going for the end of lunch. This was just as well, because what I suggested Tom should do was rude and physically impossible...

ACT 1, SCENE 3

O, *what learning is!*

(Romeo and Juliet, III. iii)

"Only another one hundred and ninety-four lunch-times left until next summer hols," announced Amy as we meandered slowly towards our first English lesson of the year with mad Mrs MacDonald. "Although it'll probably be less when you take away the days I'll be ill, one or two school trips and my Christmas shopping days off," she continued.

I shook my head. "Holidays? No thanks! I'm just glad to be back at school."

"Which proves that not only do you need a guide dog, you also need a visit to a psychiatrist!" Tom was continuing to be very annoying. "You must be the only person in the world who's pleased to be back at school. Even the teachers don't want to be back."

"*Especially* the teachers!" boomed Ms Hillier, Head of Drama, from behind us. "And will you three get to where you're going? If you go any slower, you'll grow roots! It isn't a funeral procession." She overtook us and hurtled past, her black coat and silk scarf flapping behind her, giving the impression of a giant crow swooping down the corridor, looking for carrion to feed on.

"Mind you," I said, "I didn't miss the teachers. They're all still the same."

"Yup," agreed Amy and Tom. "They should all be put away."

Judge Charlotte Robbins placed the black cap on her bewigged head and peered at the pitiful figure in the dock below her. There was a hush in the crowded courtroom as people awaited the sentence. The tension could be cut with a knife. Judge Charlotte coughed and stared the trembling wretch straight in the eyes.

"Prisoner MacDonald you have been found guilty of making bad jokes, sarcasm, shouting, giving out homework, writing 'see me!' on the bottom of essays, sending bad reports home to unsuspecting victims and generally being a pain in the neck to hundreds of unfortunate, defenceless students. I therefore sentence you to be hanged until you are very, very sorry as an example to all teachers who treat the children of this nation in such a manner. Is there anything you wish to say in your defence?"

"Why are you late?" shouted Mrs MacDonald as we wandered into our English classroom.

Here we go, I thought, more trouble. However, Tom rescued the situation by immediately blurting out his works-every-time-at-the-beginning-of-any-school-year excuse. "Sorry Miss, my new timetable said we should be in F.5, Charlie's said E6 and Amy's said the Drama Studio, but all our timetables say that we've got you, so we knew that it must be wrong, so we went to the Drama Studio and then we went to..."

"All right, all right, stop your babbling and sit down." Like a hungry fish, Mrs MacDonald gulped up the bait and was reeled in by Tom's excuse. "Damn computers! I told management that it was a ridiculous idea to trust the timetable to a computer. But would they listen to me? Oh no! 'Computers make life a lot simpler, Mrs MacDonald'. Hah! We'd be a darn sight better off without them! Did Shakespeare need a word processor? Did Dickens sit in front of a PC? Did Wordsworth need a spell checker? No, no and no!"

There was a collective glazed expression as the class let Mrs MacDonald rant on. She was a Teacher Of The Old School. Any technological advances beyond chalk and slates were considered 'far too trendy and modern'. She continued to wail and whine for several minutes before she realised that no one was taking a blind bit of notice of her. With a loud "Harumph," she changed tack and began the usual beginning-of-term pep talk.

"This is a very important subject, blah-blah; exams are very important, blah-blah; you must get homework in blah-blah; do your best or you'll regret it in the long run blah blah; I've taught lots of pupils blah-blah, who wished they'd followed my blah-blah advice instead of blah-blah messing blah-blah around, blah-blah, blah-blah, blah..."

Blah, blaaah, baaa, baaaa, baaaa.

"Come by boy!" Charlie shouted towards Rover, her trusty sheepdog, Only two more sheep to pen and she would be the One Girl and her Dog World Champion Shepherdess. Rover rounded up the two stray sheep and began to bring them down the mountainside towards the pen. Charlie peered at the descending sheep. Funny how all sheep looked like an old English teacher of hers...

"...Blah-blah, and so I hope you'll all try your very hardest and get the grades you deserve."

As I blinked awake, Mrs MacDonald continued with the obligatory 'What-I-expect-from-you" speech (*be* good, *be* quiet and *be*have) followed by a double dose of guilt ("you're responsible for your actions, and if you can't live up to those responsibilities, then you'll be letting yourselves down, not me") and moved on to the essential: "So, I hope we're going to have a happy two years together."

After we'd all smiled sweetly and nodded dumbly, she continued. "Now then, I'm sure that you'll all be excited by the fact that as part of the exam, we have to study a set play by William Shakespeare."

There was an immediate chorus of disapproval from several of the boys in the class:

"Oh no!"

"Do we have to?"

"Not Shakespeare!"

"Miss, Shakespeare's boring!"

Mrs MacDonald would have none of it. She raised herself up, threw out her arm dramatically and shouted:

"Rebellious subjects, enemies to peace,
Profaners of this neighbour stained steel -
Will they not hear? What ho - you men, you beasts..."

The class went momentarily quiet, before the mutters of "What's she on?"; "Two years of her?; and "She's a nutter!" drifted across the classroom. Mrs MacDonald ignored it all and continued. "Yes, William Shakespeare. The Swan of Avon, The Bard." She glared at the protesters. "Have you seen any Shakespeare?" she demanded. "Have you read any Shakespeare?" Grunts indicated that the protesters hadn't. "Well then how can you say it's boring, if you haven't tried it? Don't judge a book by its cover." She smiled, "And that little speech I just gave is actually from the set play. *Romeo and Juliet* - a wonderful love story."

Again there were groans from the lads. Amy turned to me, grinned and mouthed "aahhhhh, just for you!" I stuck my tongue out at her. She laughed. *Romeo and Juliet.*

It wasn't too bad. I'd seen the film. It had been brill. Romeo was played by a wispy blond Hollywood heart-throb and the lucky woman playing Juliet had had to kiss him. *And* she got paid to do it! Call that work? Life is so unfair.

"And on the subject of *Romeo and Juliet*," continued Mrs MacDonald, "I have an announcement to make. Ms Hillier has decided that this term's school production is going to be *Romeo and Juliet*. Auditions are next week in the main hall. There are more details in this week's notices and she wants as many people as possible to attend. Ooh, yes, one more thing," Mrs MacDonald peered around the class. "Ms Hillier especially asked me to say that she wants Deborah Vincent to be at the audition."

All eyes turned towards the smiling figure of Deborah. I glowered. Deborah Vincent! The incredibly popular Deborah Vincent! Not that I'm jealous of her, of course. Just because she's got bright blue eyes, long blonde shining hair, a face that could easily be on the front of magazines and a figure that made even the male teachers stare. Of course I'm not jealous of that empty-headed bimbo!

"Now after all that excitement, its time for work!" As Mrs MacDonald began to hand out our new exercise-books Amy asked me if I was going to go for the auditions. I shook my head and reminded her that I hadn't been in a school play since junior school.

"Oh yeah, the one where you forgot your lines and Mrs Hardy called you..."

"I know what she called me, thank you very much." I interrupted "After that, the thought of treading the boards leaves me cold. What about you?"

"I might," mused Amy, "it could be fun."

24

"As much fun as having your teeth pulled out without anaesthetic!"

Amy shrugged. "Well, I might go and see what's happening."

Mrs MacDonald finished handing out our books and returned to her desk. She grinned in the way that all teachers grin just before they give you some work. "Now then, in order that I can get to know you all better, I want you to write an essay for me. And I wonder if you can guess the title?"

I looked up. Surely she wasn't going to say...

"The title is... 'What I did on my holidays'."

ACT 1, SCENE 4

Hold, then. Go home, be merry...
(Romeo and Juliet, IV. i)

The full moon rose heavily over the jagged mountains of Transylvania. She stumbled on the broken path: a cold, clinging mist swirled eerily around her chilled body. In the distance she heard the howling of wolves.

She looked up. Above her loomed the terrifying ramparts of Castle Dracula. On the highest tower, a shadow moved. A gigantic vampire bat watched her approach with greedy eyes.

She approached the heavy iron-bound door, and rang the bell. She heard it chime mournfully somewhere deep within the dreadful castle. The great wooden door creaked open; trembling, she stepped through, and immediately it slammed shut behind her.

She heard the sound of footsteps. Down the magnificent marble staircase, lit only by the log fire burning in the hall, swept the Count. His cloak billowed behind him, showing a lining the colour of blood. At the bottom of the stairs he stopped, and looked at her with eyes that were windows into a world of eternal darkness. Slowly, he smiled, revealing needle-sharp fangs. She shrank back in fear; the Lord of the Vampires stepped forward, his scarlet lips quivering as he spoke the words that turned her blood to ice:

"Hello, Charlie. Good day back at school?"

"Yes, Dad." I hadn't had a good day, but there was no point saying so. Anyway, he'd already ducked into the study. Once when Dad asked me if I'd had a good day, I said, "Actually, I was run over by a bus on the way home and had to have both legs amputated below the knee", and he'd said, "Good, good," in a vague sort of way and carried on reading his case notes. Maybe my dad would listen to me if I booked a counselling session with him at work; I can't think of any other way of getting through to him.

The happy sounds of screams and thudding electronic music coming from upstairs made it a fair guess that my superbrat little brother Nick, was slaughtering aliens on his games console as usual. I could hear Mum in the kitchen, whistling a happy tune as she shoved an *Old Mother Hubberd's Genuine Olde Worlde Individual Gristle and Gravy Pie-ette (guaranteed additive-free)* in the microwave for Dad's supper.

Whenever Nick and I have a row, Mum says she spends all day sorting out other people's horrible whingeing children at school and she doesn't want to start all over again when she gets home. Then she gets her school stuff out and works on the kitchen table until half-past nine, unless she's got a council meting or one of her committees.

Our house is a bit like a railway station. It gets quite busy, but everybody is always coming in from somewhere or going out to somewhere else, nobody actually hangs around for long.

Dad came out of the study with a briefcase in one hand and his jacket in the other. He looked at me vaguely for a moment as if he couldn't quite remember who I was. "Ah, Charlie," he said as memory retrieval kicked in, "I've got to nip over to Mike's to work out where we are with the case conference tomorrow. Keep an eye on Nick, mmmm?"

I groaned. "Oh, Dad, I said I'd go over to Amy's. Why can't Mum look after Nick?"

"Child welfare committee meeting." Dad tried to balance his briefcase on his knee and open it to see he'd got all his papers. He had to hop to keep his balance. Mum came out of the kitchen and stopped in surprise.

"Roger, are you going out?"

"Just round to Mike's. Shan't be long... couple of hours or so."

"But your supper's nearly ready." She managed to make it sound as if she'd been slaving over a red-hot oven all day. "It's chicken and mushroom."

"Sorry. Bit of a last-minute panic. Charlie can eat it."

I glared at him. "I hate chicken and mushroom."

"Well, give it to Nick and make yourself a cheese sandwich or something. Got to go. Mmmmmoua!" He blew Mum a kiss that looked guaranteed to run out of steam and flop down dead on the carpet before it reached her. In the next five seconds, the microwave in the kitchen went ping, Mum yelled "Niiii-hhhiiick!" up the stairs and scampered off to get a plate out, and Dad slipped out of the front door while I stood back against the wall and waited.

With a sound like thunder, the mighty herd of buffalo swept irresistibly through the canyon. The earth shook as she cowered back against the rock, expecting at any moment to be dragged down and trampled beneath the pounding hooves of the crazed beasts...

When Nick had gone past, leaving a smoking trail in the carpet, I mooched through into the sitting-room. I was hungry, but not hungry enough to be able to stand the sight of my kid brother in a feeding frenzy. I switched the TV on. It was one of those Aussie soaps where everyone wears swimsuits around the house. One of the main characters was in a wheelchair, which was odd because I could have sworn she was perfectly OK yesterday, unless of course I was thinking of another character in a completely different soap or I'd missed an episode without realising it. It didn't matter anyway. I settled down to watch. Two and a half minutes later (slow going for him), the Creature from the Black Lagoon came through from the kitchen and slumped on the sofa. He fished a hand-held computer game console from behind a cushion and started playing with it.

"Nick, turn that off," I told him, "I can't hear the programme."

He stuck out his tongue at me and turned the sound up.

"If you don't turn the sound off, "I told him reasonably, "I shall break all your fingers."

"Ooh, scareeeyyyyyyy!"

I went across and started to pummel him. He howled. Mum came out of the kitchen. "Now what?"

Nick was curled up like an insect, which wasn't where the resemblance ended. "He won't turn the sound off," I complained. Nick writhed about on the sofa in mock agony, like a South American footballer trying to steal a penalty.

Mum rolled her eyes. "Honestly, Charlie, how old are you? It's about time you learnt to keep your fists to yourself. Say sorry to Nick."

"Sorry," I muttered, giving him the evil eye.

Mum smiled. "That's better isn't it? Now, I've got a meeting tonight, so you're in charge. I've got my mobile if there's a problem. And remember..." she pointed a finger at me, "... you get paid for babysitting so Nick gets to choose what channel or DVD to watch."

Nick gave me a smirk. It shouldn't be against the law to murder your little brother when he grins at you like that. There's no justice.

Ten minutes later Mum legged it down the path on her way to another fascinating debate about how to look after other people's children and left me with the brat. He was watching one of his DVDs. The little toad had a whole collection of Japanese *Captain Cosmos* cartoons. According to him, they were rare and valuable. He'd spend hours searching for them on the internet and then persuading mum and dad to let him buy them from special collectors from all over the world. He must of spent most of his lifetime's allowance on them. They were his pride and joy, and he watched them over and over again, which drove me spare. They were terrible: lousy stories, rotten dialogue, stupid voices, tacky drawing, one hundred per cent garbage.

"Why can't you watch the DVD on the computer?" I asked.

"Because it looks better on the TV," he replied.

"Bigger screen."

"Well, can't we watch something good?" I asked.

"This *is* good," the Pain shot back.

"No it isn't, it's just a stupid cartoon."

"It's not stupid. And it's not *just* a cartoon – it's anime. A Japanese visual art form – of course you don't know about such things, being a *girl*..."

I scowled at him. "I'm surprised you know how to speak, being a *boy*..."

Ignoring my witty repost, Nick's eyes took on a fanatical gleam. "Captain Cosmos is really Nick Goddard who had got caught in a nuclear explosion..."

I ground my teeth. "I know..."

"... and then they had to rebuild him with bionic parts and now he's a superhero who..."

"... chases baddies who all look like refugees from a circus, and they all start leaping and kung-foo fighting each other... I *know*! You've told me a dozen times already!" I realised that a different approach was called for. "But, it's just for kids."

"I *am* a kid according to you," he complained. "You keep calling me horrible little sprog and telling me how childish I am, then you moan about me watching *Captain Cosmos*. You can't have it both ways."

I realised that I wasn't going to win so I told him he was a total zonghead and ignored him. Nick had just started secondary school. Every time I saw him I felt myself cringe with embarrassment. Every time he saw me, he'd say something to one of his mates and they'd burst out laughing. Mum and Dad had even had the nerve to try and insist I walked to school with Nick, and then got all upset when I told them I'd rather be dead in a ditch.

I got out my sketch-pad and pencils, sat at the table and began to doodle.

"Charleeee! Zees is fantasteeec! You are wizout doubt, zee most breeleeant arteest een zee 'istoree of zee world!"

Charlie smiled as she thanked the President of the National Academy for his kind words. She looked up at her new painting, which was hanging in pride of place on the wall of the Louvre Museum.

The President continued to gush praise. "You are a greater arteest zan Da Vinci, Van Gogh, Picasso or Rembrandt. Zey were northeeng compared to you! Your line, your sense of colour – fantasteec! All zee world weel want zees painting. It is beyond price!"

Charlie brushed aside the compliment. "Monsieur, you are most generous, but money means nothing to me. My art is the most important thing."

"Of course, of course, but tell me, 'ooo was your inspiration, 'ooo was your model?"

I can't reveal that," replied Charlie. "I made a promise. But the clue is in the title. I call this piece...

"Garth Strong - Love God!" Nick hooted as he pointed at my sketch. I snapped out of my dream, looked down at the page, horrified and began quickly scribbling out the incriminating words.

"Garth Strong, the one in the sixth form. That Garth Strong?" He gave me an evil leer. "I bet you fancy him."

I said nothing but I could feel my face changing colour.

Nick hugged a cushion and burst into peals of laughter. "Hoohooo, hoohoo! You do! You do! My ugly sister fancies Ga-aaarth! Heeheeheeheehee!"

She shrank back in horror as the lifeless corpse slumped to the carpet. The poker slipped from her nerveless fingers and clattered into the hearth. "I've killed him," she whispered.

She tried desperately to think as blood soaked into the priceless Persian rug. She would have to bury him in the garden. She could roll him up in the rug, drag him outside, and bury him. If only she could find a spade...

I stomped out of the room, slamming the door behind me. I couldn't touch Nick and he knew it. If I knocked the stuffing out of him, he'd tell mum, and I wouldn't get my fiver, plus I'd get the Sorrowful Look and a big lecture, plus I'd be grounded.

I was still hungry, so I looked in the fridge. There wasn't any cheese, but that was OK because there wasn't any bread either. In the end, I found some microwave chips in the freezer. I gave them a spin on the magic roundabout and took them up to my room, along with some yoghurt and a pot of dip that was only a bit hairy. I put the radio on at maximum volume and lay on my bed. What a day! I stared at the ceiling and nibbled chips smeared with cheese n' onion dip and thought about Garth.

ACT 1, SCENE 5

**Love goes toward love as schoolboys from their books;
But love from love, toward school with heavy looks.**
(Romeo and Juliet, II.ii)

School was pretty dull over the next few days. I did my double detention with Mr Brooks and kept my head down. All the lessons seemed to be made up of new books being given out, speeches about the importance of exams and being lectured on the topic of Being Responsible and Mature. I was beginning to think that Amy and Tom were right about school holidays when it happened.

On Friday lunch-time, Amy asked me to help her learn some lines for the audition. By the time we'd finished and we'd got to the school canteen all the burgers, chips and beans had gone and all that was left was the sort of healthy food that no one else wanted: shepherd's pie, fish casserole and green vegetables - yuck! Honestly! Amy decided to risk the fish, but I had a craving for grease, so I nipped down to the chippy for a battered sausage.

It took me ages and I had to run back to school to get back in time for registration. As I pelted along the empty corridors, a figure stepped out of a doorway right in front of me. I tried to screech to a halt, but couldn't. I crashed into the shape and was sent spinning to the floor. My bag spilt open and my books went flying across the corridor. I looked up to see who I was about to give a mouthful of abuse to when my mouth clammed shut and my legs went all kind of wobbly. Towering above me was GARTH!

Her body dangled over the cliff. She could hear the roar of the river far, far below. She felt her grip on the broken branch getting weaker. It was no good. She couldn't hold on any longer.

Suddenly a face appeared over the edge of the cliff. It was Garth!

"Reach up!" he ordered in his strong, manly voice. He reached down. She reached up. Their fingers met just as the branch split and fell into the depths of the canyon. Only the tight grip of Garth's hand was stopping her plunging to her

certain death.

"Hang on," he rasped. "I've got you!" With gritted teeth and muscles rippling in the breeze, he slowly pulled her up, inch by inch towards the safety of his muscled arms...

"Watch out, you could have hurt me!" Garth complained.

"Er, sorry." I began scrabbling around the floor, picking my books up and trying not to look so stupid.

"You made me drop my book!" I looked at the book he was pointing at and quickly picked it up. *Romeo and Juliet*!

"Er, are, er, are you going to go to the auditions for the school play?" I stammered as I handed the book back to him.

"Oh no," he said carelessly. "I don't need to. Ms Hillier's already told me that she wants me to play Romeo. Thanks." He took the book, turned and marched off leaving me sitting on the floor. I licked my lips as I watched him disappear into the distance. I may have slobbered a bit as well. "Romeo, Romeo, wherefore art thou Romeo?" I called out. There was a laugh from behind me. I swivelled round to see Nick and his year seven cronies pointing at me and laughing. The dreaded blush began to flare.

"Shut it!" I growled unconvincingly. They carried on laughing.

"Is that your sister?" one of them asked Nick. I stared daggers at the brat as he nodded yes.

"You're right, she is mad."

"I think I might go to that audition next week," I told Amy as we trudged home.

"You!" she exclaimed.

"Yes. Me. What's wrong with that?" I replied in my best 'hurt' voice.

Amy was gazing at me with a mixture of shock and amusement. "I thought that you hated acting. 'Worse than going to the dentist', you said."

"Yes, well I've changed my mind. Aren't I allowed to? I think it will be good for me. I think I should try and get over this fear by facing up to it and tackling it head-on," I said dramatically.

Amy nodded. "Sorry, it's just that... you know... sorry."

There was a pause as we carried on walking.

"What part are you thinking of going for?"

"Juliet."

Amy's eyes narrowed. "You've found out, haven't you?" she said.

I could feel my cheeks beginning to prick. "What's that supposed to mean?" I said defensively.

"Oh, leave it out, Charlie." Amy had a fit of the giggles while I tried to decide whether disembowelling her or boiling her in oil would be more fun. "You're suddenly interested in the audition because you've found out that Garth has been cast as Romeo."

"How do you know he's going to be Romeo?" I asked.

"It's common knowledge," Amy replied. "Everyone knows. He's doing A level theatre arts, Hillier thinks he's the bees knees and he's been going round all week boasting that he doesn't have to audition because he's got the main part! Everyone's known for ages."

"Well, I didn't until today..."

"Aha!" Amy grinned at me. "Found out!"

"That's got nothing to do with it!" I told her hotly. "I don't organise my life around whether some lad might or might not fancy me."

Amy nodded solemnly. "If you say so."

"Anyway, I don't fancy him. I want to do the play because it's a set book, and everyone says the best way to get to know a play is to act in it, and if I'm going to do it anyway I might as well try for Juliet, and if anything happens between me and Garth because of the play..."

"Oho!"

"... I said *if*, that's just whatsit. Fate or something. It's not that I want to do the play because of Garth..."

"Right, right."

"... it's the call of the greasepaint, the smell of the stage."

"You wouldn't want to smell of our stage," Amy told me. "Not after the dance club have been doing a work-out in sweaty bare feet. You'd put Garth right off you."

"I told you I'm not interested in Garth. Why do you automatically assume I want to do Juliet just on the off-chance that Garth might finally notice I'm alive and start to fancy me? Anyway, why shouldn't Garth fancy me? What's wrong with me?"

"You're shouting."

I was about to tell her I wasn't shouting when I realised that several heads were turned in our direction. I turned instant red, bit my lips and looked hard at my shoes.

"Look," said Amy supportively, "I think it's brilliant that you're going to go for the audition, whether it's because of Garth or not, OK?"

I nodded a yes and felt a bit ashamed. Amy had been

right, but she didn't make anything of it. I ~~was~~ having her as a friend. She was so sorted o~~ut~~ about everything. Ask her a question and perfect answer. Need some support, and s~~he~~ of-the-range crutch lined up ready and waiting. ~~She was~~ best Best Friend that anyone could have.

"Er, sorry," I mumbled. "For shouting..."

"No probs," she replied. "Have a good weekend - and get learning those lines!"

The drum rolls sounded as Charlie 'The Memory' Robbins built up to the climax of her act.

"What is the thirty second name on page seventy-five of the1965 edition of the London telephone book?" asked the man in the audience.

"I wish you'd chosen a harder one," laughed the world's greatest memory expert. "It is Bull. S. 25 Acacia Gardens. 01 242343464575696707."

"Correct!"

The cymbals crashed and the audience went into a frenzy of cheering and wild applause.

"Romeo, Romeo! Wherefore art thou, Romeo? Deny thy name and refuse thy father...."

"No, it's 'Deny thy father and refuse thy name', not the other way round..." corrected Mum, looking at our family edition of *The Complete Works of Shakespeare* which she'd got off the lounge bookshelf (where it had stood untouched for years and years). "Are you sure you want to do this dear?"

"Yes, of course," I snapped. "The audition's on Monday and I've got to be word perfect if I'm going to get art."

Mum sighed deeply. "OK, start again."

Mum had volunteered to help me go through my lines after a sustained campaign of nagging and sulking by me. Dad had refused point blank ("Haven't got the time. I've got to go to a seminar on Neglected Teenagers.") and there was no way I was getting Nick to help, so Mum had eventually decided to take on the role of Interested and Supportive Parent.

After another fifteen minutes of fluffs and total blanks, mum was definitely showing signs of restlessness. "Is that about it? I've got a meeting soon and I've still got to go shopping..."

"It's not my fault," I snapped. "It's Shakespeare's! Why couldn't he write in normal English instead of using words that people have never heard of?"

Mum just smiled and said patronisingly. "Yes, dear. As you say. Shall we carry on...?"

By the end of the weekend I felt pretty confident about the part. I could struggle through Juliet's famous speech and give some sort of meaning to it (even if I still didn't know exactly what the hell she was gabbling on about). I'd also phoned Amy loads of times, asking for her advice, like, "Because Juliet was getting ready for bed, should I wear my nightie for the audition?" ("Not a good idea."), "Should I walk around a lot throwing my arms about?" ("No, because it's a balcony scene and you might fall off it.") and "Would it be a good idea if I hugged a teddy bear, pretend it was Romeo and talk to it?" ("No. Teddy bears weren't around in 16th century Italy and it would look stupid"). I didn't tell Amy that I often talked to my bear and pretended it was Garth.

I'd also bought the *Romeo and Juliet* DVD and watched in three times (thus annoying Grot Brot by stopping him watching his stupid *Captain Cosmos* cartoons – ha, ha). I'd taken some notes about how to play the scene, although I wasn't sure how I could copy the bit where Romeo and Juliet end up in a swimming pool (I looked at the play script and discovered that Shakespeare didn't actually mention a swimming pool). I was as prepared as I could be.

As I got ready for bed on Sunday I stood in front of the mirror and looked myself straight in the eye. "Right, Charlie, you can do it," I told myself. "Go and get that part. Go and get your man..."

ACT 2

ACT 2, SCENE 1

Hear me with patience but to speak a word...
(Romeo and Juliet, III.v)

"And the winner is... Charlie Robbins for ROMEO AND JULIET!

She clapped one immaculately manicured hand over her mouth in well-feigned shock; of course she knew she would get the Best Actress Oscar, it was a foregone conclusion, but she had to act surprised and delighted. It was what the audience expected.

She tripped lightly into the stage. With the golden statuette in her hand, she turned a brilliant smile on the audience.

"Gee, I never dreamed..." She managed to squeeze out several tears. "This is one of the greatest honours any actress can ever have, no matter how incredibly good she is. I want to thank you all for voting for me, and for all your good wishes. As you know, Garth Strong, who is my Romeo, not only in the film, but in real life..." (She had to pause for a moment as cheers and applause rang out round the hall: back at her table she could see people congratulating Garth and telling him how lucky he was.) "...Garth and I are shortly to be married..." (Renewed cheering broke out.) "And in conclusion, I'd like to thank all the little people who helped me to create not only the greatest movie in cinema history, but the greatest performance of Juliet ever seen..."

"Next!"

I sat up with a jerk. Amy was walking off the stage. It was my turn. Ms Hillier looked over her shoulder. "Next! Who's next? Oh... Charlie."

I stood up. My chair tipped over with a crash. Ms Hillier sighed. I set off towards the stage. It was like walking to the scaffold. I climbed up the steps at the side of the stage and walked hesitantly to the middle. Ms Hillier sat at a table in the middle of the hall, with the other auditionees straggling out in rows to either side of her. She was scribbling a note. I would have bet money she was only doing it to put me off.

Ms Hillier was another of the main reasons I'd never really done much in drama. She had favourites, for one thing, and I wasn't one of them. Then there were the mood swings. She was up one minute, bubbling with enthusiasm, bursting with energy... and the next minute, she'd be a heap of misery going on about the Tragedy of the Human Condition and making us do grim little improvisations about eating disorders and suicide. She was short and plumpish and had hair that caused hardened stylists to burst into tears. She always dressed in plain black except for a scarf. She told us once, during one of her darker moments, that she wore the scarf in memory of Isadora Duncan, and then went into a sulk when we said we'd never heard of her. Apparently this Duncan woman was a famous dancer who died tragically when the long scarf she always wore got caught round the back wheel of a car she was travelling in and romantically broke her neck. This sounded to me pretty daft (and morbid) reason to wear a scarf, but Ms Hillier was like that. She never wore makeup but she painted her nails (fingers and toes).

A lot of the people she taught worshipped her. The rest of us thought she was mad.

She finished writing her note and looked up without enthusiasm. "What are you going to read for us, Charlie?"

I took a deep breath. "Juliet."

A spasm of pain crossed Ms Hillier's face. Behind

her, someone sniggered in an unsupportive sort of way.

"Very well, Charlie." Ms Hillier gave me what she probably thought was an encouraging smile. "In your own time."

I took a deep breath. "*Oh, Romeo, Romeo, wherefore art thou, Romeo?...*"

I stopped, appalled. I sounded like Minnie Mouse on helium.

Somebody behind Ms Hillier laughed. Right, I thought.

"*Oh, Romeo, Romeo! wherefore art thou, Romeo?*
Deny thy father and refuse thy name..."

At the end of the speech, Ms Hillier blinked and said, "Thank you, Charlie." She sounded surprised. Thanks for the vote of confidence, I thought.

I trudged back to my chair. My face was going critical. I sat down next to Amy, who gave me a grin and the thumbs-up. I glared at her.

"And what are you going to give us, Deborah?"

My hackles rose and I looked back at the stage. Deborah Vincent had taken the stage stood facing Ms Hillier. She looked graceful, poised and confident. I wanted to kill her.

"Juliet, miss."

There was a sigh of appreciation from Ms Hillier. I glanced at Amy. She rolled her eyes.

"*Oh, Romeo! Romeo!*" Deborah turned eyes like soup plates on the audience. "*Wherefore art thou. Romeo?...*"

Deborah's face suddenly became distorted with terror.

43

"You..." she choked, "... put something in the wine!"

Charlie gave her a merciless grin. "A little concoction of my own. Arsenic mixed with strychnine, belladonna, rat poison and sulphuric acid. At last, you shall suffer the fate you deserve. Revenge is mine!"

The evil Deborah clasped her throat, gasping for breath as her black and swollen tongue burst horribly between her bloodless lips...

"...and for thy name, which is no part of thee,
Take all myself."

Deborah struck a pose and beamed at the audience. There was a pattering of applause.

"Very good, Deborah," gushed Ms Hillier. She turned to the rest of us. "Thank you all very much," she said. "We'll let you know."

Amy had zoomed off to see her dad immediately after the audition, so it wasn't until lunch-time the next day that we were able to hold an inquest.

"Three times," Amy hooted. "She forgot her words three times!"

I slumped against the wire mesh of the tennis courts. "She'll still get it."

"Oh, come on!" Amy stared at me. "Hillier can't give Juliet to Deborah. You saw her. She can't act and she's got the brains of a fish."

"She looks the part though."

"Looks aren't everything," said Amy automatically.

"They are if you want anyone to take you seriously

in drama."

"Well, people might take *you* more seriously if you didn't spend every drama lesson hiding at the back trying not to be noticed."

Amy huffed off to talk to Tom and I put in a few minutes practice for the All England National Sulking Championships. Then I mooched over to them.

"Sorry," I muttered. "I mean, who cares who plays Juliet...?"

The door of the science block flung open, and Garth came out. Hot and cold shivers ran all over me. I forgot to breathe as I watched him cross the yard.

"Right. Who cares?" said Amy.

I swung round on Tom. "What are you grinning at?"

"Oh come on," he smirked. "You were staring at Garth like our dog eyeing up the postman's leg!"

"I *was* not!"

"You were," said Amy, "and then you sighed like a vacuum cleaner running down..."

The bell went for the second lunch sitting.

"Hey, heads up, gang. It's swill time!" Tom raced off towards the dining-hall to grab a place at the front of the line. Amy and I followed more slowly.

"Well, I think they should give you Juliet." Amy took me by the arm. "You read very well."

"They won't though. They'll give it to Deborah." I tossed my head and wished my hair would fly around defiantly like Deborah's did. "Anyway, it doesn't matter. It's like Ms Hillier says, when you do a play you're a company of actors working together. It's not about who has the most lines."

"Does she say that?"

"Yes, she does. And she says there're no such things

as small parts, only small actors. So I don't care what I play."

"Peter!?"

I stared at the cast list in horror. My name was right at the bottom against a character I'd never even heard of.

"Peter? Who the hell's Peter?"

"He's a servant, I think." Amy's head was next to mine as she studied the list.

"But it's a tiny part," I wailed. "*And* it's a man!"

Amy lifted an eyebrow. "I thought you said you didn't care..."

I felt my face going red again. "Oh, it's all right for you. You've got the nurse. That's what you read for, isn't it?"

Amy was leafing through her copy of the play. "Look, it's OK. Peter is the Nurse's serving-man." She gave me a big bright smile. "You're playing my servant. That'll be nice, won't it?"

"Oh, absolutely great. Just peachy. Thanks a heap."

Amy sniffed. "Please yourself. I just thought it would be nice if we had some scenes together. There's no need to get at me, I didn't cast the stupid play."

"Sorry." I stared at the cast list. "I'm glad you got the part you wanted, honestly."

Amy sighed. "Yeah."

I looked hard at her. "Am I missing something? You got the part you went for, didn't you?"

"I went for the part I thought I could get. That's not the same thing as getting the part you wanted."

I couldn't think of anything to say to that. I looked back to the two names at the top of the cast list:

46

Romeo .... Garth Strong
Juliet .... Deborah Vincent

I realised that Amy was looking at the same names. She caught me looking at her and turned away quickly.

Tom wandered up. "You two got your parts, then?" He looked at the list. He looked at me. "Who's Peter when he's at home?"

"Well, we know who we are now," Amy said brightly. "I suppose we'd better start learning our lines."

I snorted. "That isn't going to take me very long."

ACT 2, SCENE 2

My dismal scene I needs must act alone...
(Romeo and Juliet, IV.iii)

"Nurse, where's my daughter?
Call her forth to me..."

"Stop!" Ms Hillier snapped her book shut in irritation. "Emma, what are you doing?"

Emma Wicks, the sixth former who was playing Lady Capulet, straightened up. "Sorry, miss?"

Ms Hillier ran harassed fingers through her hair. "Emma, you don't need to come hobbling on with a stick..."

"I thought it would help me to feel the character..."

"...and you don't need to mutter and mumble away like Little Red Riding Hood's granny. Juliet is fourteen years old, for pity's sake, and Lady Capulet says earlier that she had her when she wasn't much older herself. You may be the wrong side of thirty but you're not geriatric. Lose the stick." She opened her book again. "From the top..."

"Nurse, where's my daughter?
Call her forth to me."

Amy came bustling on and gave her first line.

"Now, by my maidenhead at twelve year old..."

She stopped. "Miss, is that supposed to be a joke?"

Ms Hillier groaned. "It implies that she lost her maidenhead when she was thirteen. All right?"

"What's maidenhead, miss?" asked Amy, knowing perfectly well.

Ms Hillier ground her teeth. "Virginity."

"Oh. So it's meant to be rude." Amy thought for a moment. "Should I wait for a laugh?"

"Just get on with it!"

"Now, by my maidenhead at twelve year old,
I bade her come. What, lamb! What, ladybird!
God forbid! Where's this girl? What, Juliet!"

Deborah tripped on from the side of the stage. She stopped dead, leant theatrically towards Amy, cupped a hand round her ear and trilled,

"How now, who calls?"

"Oh, God!" Ms Hillier fumbled the top off a small

brown bottle, shook a tablet out and swallowed it.

I slumped down in my seat. Rehearsals are weird. I'd never really been involved in one before. When you see a finished play, you sort of take the scenery and costume and lights and things for granted. Listening to everybody speaking Shakespeare's strange, rolling lines on a bare stage, wearing their everyday clothes, under bright strip lighting... well, it was weird. Like Amy wasn't exactly Amy, and she wasn't exactly the Nurse. She was somewhere in between, looking like one and talking like the other. Spooky.

"How's it going?" Tom appeared at my shoulder. I jumped.

"What are you doing here? You're not in the play."

"Not *performing* in the play. I said I'd help make the props."

"You don't need to watch rehearsals to do that." I gave him a ferocious scowl. "Anyway, I wouldn't want to use any prop you made."

Tom looked hurt. "Why not?"

"Because you're useless at making things. Look at that spice rack you made in woodwork."

"Nothing wrong with that spice rack."

"No, except it was supposed to be a bookcase only you got the measurements wrong."

"Could have happened to anybody," he protested.

We watched the stage for a bit. Tom yawned and then looked guilty.

"Amy's good, isn't she?"

"Hmmm."

"Deborah's terrible, though."

"Oh, I don't know." I put on a thoughtful expression. "She does have that film-star look."

Tom looked surprised. "What, you mean like Marilyn Monroe?"

"I was thinking more of E.T."

He grinned. "You been on yet?"

"They haven't got to my bit." My eyes wandered along the row of chairs to where Garth was sitting, waiting for his next scene.

The King of the Jungle swung athletically onto the branch where she waited with bated breath. "AAAAAAAEEEAAAAAAEEEEEEAAAAAAAHHH!"

He gazed at her in puzzlement, as she lay at his mercy. Man and beast were clearly at war within his powerfully-muscled body, which was naked except for a leopard-skin loin cloth. Staring down at her with melting eyes, he raised one powerful hand and clapped it to his mighty chest. "Me Tarzan."

Helpless before his animal magnetism, she murmured, "Me Jane..."

"You really have got the hots for old 'I-Love-Me-Who-Do-You-Love', haven't you?" Tom was watching me with his arms folded.

I gave him a dirty look and a sniff. "What's the matter - jealous?"

"I'm not jealous, I'm just interested. You see, I've got this theory."

"Oh yes? Go on, then."

"What I reckon is, you ask any girl what sort of person she wants to go out with, and she'll say she wants a nice dependable type who's considerate and understanding and all that."

"With you so far."

"Only... if this girl actually met a bloke like that, she wouldn't have him as a gift, because what she *really* wants is a muscle-bound dimbo sex god with pecs you could crack rocks on. Even if she knows he'll treat her like dirt and dump her for someone else inside a month."

I gave him a pitying smile. "Nice theory. Of course, it applies equally to boys."

Tom looked shocked. "You reckon?"

"Boys don't care about personality, all they want is looks and curvy bits. Of course, Garth isn't like that," I quickly added.

Tom shook his head in disbelief. "Give me one good reason why you should fancy him."

"He's good-looking, he's clever and he's a sixth-former."

"That's three reasons, I only asked for one." Tom sat back. "I just don't get it. There're loads of nicer blokes to fancy."

"Name one," I challenged.

He said, not looking in my direction, "Well... me, for instance."

"You?!"

"Why not?" he shot back. "And don't say you don't like me, we're always talking and having a laugh. Ever since junior school."

I shook my head in exasperation. "Tom, of course I *like* you; but I can't *fancy* you. You're not a real man. You're a friend."

Tom didn't say anything for a moment. Then he stood up and gave me a sickly grin. "I'll take that as a compliment."

I realised that I'd got my foot stuck so far in my

big mouth, I could chew on my ankle. "Yes, well... just stop going on about Garth."

"Right. Right. I suppose I'd better go and make some props... or something." He wandered off with his shoulders slumped.

"Go, girl, seek happy nights to happy days."

Amy finished her scene with a flourish and whisked Deborah off stage. Benvolio and Mercutio bounced on and started being laddish all over the place. Amy came and sat down by me.

"We're on in a minute." She took off a trainer and massaged her foot. When I didn't say anything, she gave me a sidelong glance. "What did Tom want?"

I gave her a rundown of our recent conversation. She was looking a bit thoughtful by the time I'd finished. She didn't say anything. Eventually I asked, "Do you think I upset him?"

"Well, I don't suppose you made his day."

"I didn't mean to hurt his feelings. I've just never thought of Tom like that. I couldn't go out with him. I mean, can you imagine kissing Tom? It would be like kissing my grandad."

Amy stared at me. "Well, you do kiss your grandad."

"Yes, but I don't stick my tongue down his throat."

Amy shrugged. "Fair point."

I bit my lip. "Do you think I should try to explain?"

"Would you like me to have a word with him?"

Amy the peacemaker. She was always sorting out the problems my big mouth caused. "Thanks. You're a pal."

"Here comes Romeo, here comes Romeo."

Benvolio and Mercutio stood eagerly gazing off into the wings while Garth came on from the other side. When they'd got that sorted out, he spoke his first line:

"Good morrow to you both. What counterfeit did I give you?"

I bit my lip and squeezed Amy's arm so hard she gave a yelp and snatched it away. I just sat there and watched Garth, and melted. His voice washed over me in waves. I didn't understand a word he was saying... he kept going on about geese for some reason... but the sound of his voice turned me into a jellyfish. I don't know how long Amy had been tugging at my sleeve before I came to.

She was dragging me out of my chair. "Earth calling Charlie. Come in, Charlie. We're on."

She swanned onto the stage with me dragging along behind her feeling like a spare part. I gave Garth a cheesy grin - a complete waste of time as he had his nose buried in his script.

It wasn't much of a scene. Amy and I had rehearsed it by ourselves at lunch-time. Basically, the Nurse comes on to talk to Romeo, and Mercutio and Benvolio take the mickey out of her while Peter (i.e. me) stands around being left out and feeling like a lemon. As this is the story of my life, I didn't really need to act.

"Peter!"

Amy dug me savagely in the ribs with her elbow and said, "Peter," again. I blinked and looked at my script. Here it was, my big line. I squared my shoulders, cleared my throat, threw out my chest and said:

"Anon."

And that was it for about three pages. I just stood there feeling stupid while Mercutio and Benvolio took the mickey out of Amy. My mind started to wander.

His eyes smouldering like burning coals, Garth clasped her to his heaving bosom and declared his passion in Shakespeare's greatest love scene:

Romeo	*Oh Charlie! Charlie, sweet! Where art thou, chuck?*
Juliet	*Oh, I am here, thou great big gorgeous hunk!*
Romeo	*Then let me taste thy lips as sweet as wine.*
Juliet	*Aye, snog me 'til I faint, for thou art mine!*

"Charlie!"

I came to with a jolt. Ms Hillier was looking at me as if I was something the cat had dragged in.

"Charlie, you've only got three lines in this scene and two of those are 'Anon'. Is there any chance you could keep your mind on the rehearsal long enough to say them?"

Amy gave me a sympathetic grimace. Garth raised his eyebrows at me. I went into my world famous beetroot imitation.

Ms Hillier snorted. "Give her the cue again, Amy."

"And thou must stand by too, and suffer every knave to use me at his pleasure?"

"I saw no man use you at his pleasure..."

Three lines later I went back to staring at space and waiting for the incredible thrill of getting to say "Anon" again at the end of the scene (which Ms Hillier had to take at a gallop because the caretaker came in looking at his watch and moaning that we'd have to clear out for the step-aerobics class).

Oh, the glamour of the theatre!

ACT 2, SCENE 3

My blood for your rude brawls doth lie a-bleeding...
(Romeo and Juliet, III. i)

Tom hailed me from across the yard. "Hi, Charlie! Are you rehearsing tonight?"

I shrugged. We hadn't actually done any of my scenes for over a week, but I'd tagged along to rehearsals with Amy and filled in for people who were away. So far I'd played An Old Man, Friar John, Balthasar, First Citizen; First Serving-man, Second Serving-man (both at the same time until Ms Hillier said watching me having a conversation with myself was making her head ache, and made Tom read one of the parts) and Third Serving-man; A Page, An Officer, An Apothecary; and enough Gentlemen and Gentlewomen of Both Houses to fill a football ground. I'd even done five minutes of Mercutio when Jason was late from football practice.

"Davis says we can make the daggers in technology this afternoon. I'm staying after school to get them finished.

Like to give me a hand?"

I shrugged again. "I don't mind." Anything was better than going home and being Responsible for Nick. The play was a good excuse, even if I wasn't getting anywhere with Garth. Which I wasn't.

We headed along the corridor towards the workshops when Ms Hillier came barging out of the staffroom and sideswiped me into the lockers.

"Oh, sorry, Charlie." She looked flustered, even for her. "Have either of you two seen Deborah this morning? She wasn't in English."

Amy breezed up in time to catch the last bit. "She's away, miss. One of the prefects brought a note round to say she's rung in sick."

"Damn!" Ms Hillier bit her lip. "I don't know how we're going to rehearse the parting scene tonight. We really should have understudies for the main characters."

I tried to keep my voice casual as I said, "I could do that, miss."

Ms Hillier completely failed to prevent a spasm of horror from flitting across her face. "You, Charlie? Understudy Juliet?" She shuddered. "Oh, well, I don't suppose it can't do any harm... but it's a thankless task, you know, you'll have to learn a lot of lines and the chances are you'll never get to play the part."

"I don't mind, miss."

She shook her head. "Oh, well, you can read in for Deborah tonight, anyway, I suppose."

She trotted off to make somebody else feel inadequate. Tom and Amy were staring at me. After a moment, Amy said, matter-of-factly, "The parting scene. Isn't that the scene where Romeo and Juliet have just... you know..."

"Slept together," Tom put in helpfully.

"Yes... and they're saying goodbye to each other and there's loads of kissing and cuddling and stuff?"

"Oh, is there?" I said unconvincingly. "Look, I'll catch you up in a minute, OK?"

I ducked into the girls' toilet, slammed the cubicle door, leaned back against it, and punched the air three times.

"Yes! Yesss!! YYYESSS!!!"

I spent the afternoon looking at the clock every five minutes. Time dragged by. At last, I had Garth where I wanted him! A passionate love scene! I'd give him passionate. If I made a mess of the lines a few times, I reckoned I could spin it out to half an hour, minimum. Plenty of time for me to give Garth a snogging he wouldn't forget in a hurry.

By the time we got to the last class of the day, technology, I was feeling ready to wrestle a tiger.

The prop daggers were almost complete. I'd promised Tom I'd help him with them, so he showed me how to cover the handles with rubber solution and then wind string around round them so that it lay in a neat spiral. Then we had to paint more glue over the top of the string. It was a nice easy job, the sort of thing that even Tom couldn't make a mess of. I'd've found it relaxing myself if I hadn't been coiled up like an overwound spring.

Amy came over, picked up a dagger and inspected it critically. "It's a bit blunt, isn't it?"

Tom gave her an exasperated look. "It's meant to be blunt. You can't have actors stabbing each other."

Amy put the dagger down, then stared at her hand in disgust. "Oh, yuck! The handle's all sticky."

"Of course it is. I've only just glued it. Don't do that!"

Amy paused in the act of absent-mindedly wiping her gluey hand on her pullover. "What?"

"That's rubber glue. Once you've got it on your clothes it'll never come out."

Amy gazed in horror at the white smear on her pullover. "Why didn't you tell me?"

"I did."

"I meant before! You never warned me the handle was wet!"

"You could see us working on them. You shouldn't be over here anyway."

I glared over my shoulder at them. "Will you two put a sock in it? I'm trying to concentrate."

Amy ignored me. "Look at this! And it's all your fault." She gave Tom a shove.

Tom fell back into me.

The craft knife I was about to use to cut the string sliced into my thumb.

Everything stopped.

I stared stupidly at my thumb. Blood was spurting out of it; not pouring, but pulsing with my heartbeat, and splashing on the bench.

I began to feel very light-headed.

"Oh, God; Charlie, Charlie, I'm sorry." Amy looked pale. She put an arm around me. Tom called for Mr Davis, who came over with a resigned look on his face.

"What is it now? Somebody can't keep their fingers out of the way?" He looked more closely and grimaced; then he became very brisk and professional. "All right. Dawn, nip over to the first-aid room and ask the school nurse to come across, would you? Tell her what's happened. Come and sit down, Charlie." He led me to a stool. Amy came with me. She still had her arm round me.

Mr Davis went to the first-aid box on the wall and came back wearing blue throw-away gloves and carrying a pad of white material. "Now, just hold this and squeeze tight to stop the bleeding until we can get you to casualty. You'll probably need a couple of stitches in there."

I was feeling more light-headed and weird by the minute. From nowhere, a line from *Romeo and Juliet* popped into my head.

"*Ay, ay, a scratch,*" I said airily, and giggled. "*Marry, 'tis enough.*"

It was one of Mercutio's lines, after he's been wounded by Tybalt. Amy goggled at me. Mr Davis clearly thought I was having hysterics. "Calm down, Charlie, it's not that serious."

I giggled again. "*No, 'tis not so deep as a well, nor so wide as a church door, but 'tis enough, 'twill serve.*"

I though I heard Mr Davis mutter, "Delirious," but just then the door opened and Garth came in.

"Excuse me," he said, "but is Charlie Robbins here? Ms Hillier asked me to..." He suddenly saw me, and stopped dead.

She lay on the crisp white hospital sheets, feeling her life ebbing away. He stood by her bedside, tying his stethoscope into knots in an agony of indecision.

"Dear Heaven, Charlie," he whispered brokenly, "don't ask me to operate on you. I can't do it!"

She fixed him with eyes that were dim with pain. "You're the finest surgeon in the world, Garth. If you can't do it, no-one can. Don't tell me you've never taken a chance and performed a hideously risky, insanely dangerous untried operation before!"

"But that was different!" he wailed. "Sure, I've taken chances when it was do or die, kill or cure, win or lose… but those were just patients, strangers. I can't take that sort of a chance with you, Charlie." He swallowed hard. "I guess you just mean too goddam much to me."

With the last of her feeble strength, she seized his hand in hers.

"Garth, you're my only hope. My life is in your hands." Her eyes closed. "Do it," she whispered.

I opened my eyes again and looked at Garth. He was staring at the blood. On the bench. On the floor. Soaking through the pressure pad I was holding to my thumb.

His eyes rolled up in his head and he slid to the floor in a dead faint.

"Oh, Lord, not another one," said Mr Davis. "Loosen his clothes, somebody."

Every girl in the class rushed to obey.

I think I would have tried to fight them off, but just then Dawn came back with the nurse. Before I knew where I was, I was being wrapped in a blanket and bundled into a wheelchair by an angel of mercy with the muscles of a lady wrestler. I couldn't believe it! There was Garth stretched out on the floor with Mr Davis trying to explain that he didn't need all his clothes loosening by *quite* so many people, and I was being wheeled off with Amy stumbling behind me carrying my jacket and my bag and crying with shock: and five minutes earlier I'd been looking forward to a passionate love scene with Garth! I tried to get out of the chair.

"I'm fine," I shrilled.

A hand like a vice pulled me back down. "Calm down, lovie."

"It's only a nick!"

"I've got my car here. We'll have you sorted out in a jiffy."

"Can't you just put an Elastoplast on it?"

"Let's make you comfy, then."

"It's nearly stopped bleeding, look…!"

The car door slammed on me and I was whisked off to the hospital, and away from Garth.

I was in casualty for three hours. After a while, my thumb started to hurt really badly and I began to feel sick. I soon got tired of listening to Amy apologise. Another nurse put some of those butterfly strips over the cut, and a bandage on my thumb that was so big that it stuck up in the air and made me look as if I was holding a giant ice-cream cone.

I hoped for a while that they'd bring Garth in too, and I could soothe his fevered brow etc. but in the morning Tom told me they'd just dribbled cold water down his back until he woke up and then sent him home and cancelled the rehearsal.

Deborah was back next day.

ACT 3

ACT 3, SCENE 1

Wilt thou be gone?

(Romeo and Juliet, III. v)

Despite having to wear the thumb bandage for a couple of weeks, I didn't get any time off of school. I also didn't get any sympathy from the family. It took Dad three days to realise what I'd done; Mum had said it was my own stupid fault (wrong - it was Tom and Amy's stupid faults) and Nick thought it was hilarious to keep asking: "Are you all right?" and giving me the thumbs-up sign (I gave him a different sign when Mum wasn't looking).

Sympathy from the teachers was totally out of the question and because it wasn't my writing hand that had been injured, I still had to do all my schoolwork and homework. Honestly, what's the point in being injured if you can't have time off school? The only thing I managed to get out of doing was PE, which isn't a great achievement - anyone with half a brain can get out of doing PE.

The play rehearsals were still progressing. Even my untrained eye could tell that it was beginning to look more like a play, rather than a load of unconnected scenes. Some things were still the same though. Deborah was still awful, I was still filling in for loads of people and Garth still wasn't aware of my existence.

During the last rehearsal before the half-term holiday, Amy and I were grimacing as we witnessed Deborah murdering Shakespeare's poetry by delivering it a nasal monotone, whilst Ms Hillier pulled out what little hair she'd got left.

"You're supposed to be in love, not speaking like a Dalek, for pity's sake. Give the lines some expression; *please*!"

"What are you doing for half-term?" Amy asked as Deborah droned on in the background.

"Huh," I grunted. "The same as I did for summer. Nothing."

"Oh right." Amy looked down at her feet. There was something obviously bothering her. She wasn't telling me something.

"I know you're not revealing everything. Call it a hunch or something, but I know." Charlotte Robbins, top interrogator for MI6 smiled as she turned the light to shine straight into the shifty eyes of the sweating figure cowering before her.

"So Amy, you will tell me the truth. I know you're lying. You know who the spy is. And I know that you know. And you know that I know that you know. And I know that you know that I know that you know who the spy is, so you'll save us both a lot of time if you just tell me..."

"I can't," sobbed Amy.

"In that case, we have other ways of making you talk..."

"So what are we going to do over half-term?" I asked.

"Er, sorry, I'm not going to be around," muttered Amy. "I'm going away."

"Away? Again?" I was shocked and a bit annoyed. "But I thought we could go down town shopping and see some movies and watch DVDs and things. Like we *usually* do at half-terms..."

"Yeah, sorry," apologised Amy. "But you know Mum and Dad were fighting over who could take me skiing at Christmas? Well Mum won. But Dad said I could only go with mum if he can take me to the Canary Islands at half-term. So I've got to go."

Unbelievable, I thought. If only my Mum and Dad would have those sorts of arguments!

"It's just their way," Amy continued. "You know what they're like. I just have to let them get on with it. It helps them with their guilt."

I nodded. "Parents, who'd have them!"

"Actually, they had you," interrupted Tom as crept up behind us. "You see, when your daddy's sperm, met your mummy's egg..."

"Thank you Tom," Amy laughed. "We've all done biology..."

"... So you can get lost," I smiled venomously. I still hadn't forgiven him for the craft knife incident.

"Ooooh, you're in an A-double-plus good mood, I think not," Tom observed sarcastically. "What's wrong with her?" he asked Amy, nodding towards me.

"Nothing is wrong with *her*," I replied pointedly. "Apart from: a) I've got a rubbish part in the play, b) Garth still doesn't know that I actually exist and c) my best friend is leaving me once again during holiday time, so I've got nothing to do other than put up with my brother, who I will probably have to look after because my mother and father will more than likely be at meetings, lectures, courses or seminars learning all about how to deal with other people's problems."

There was a pause as Tom pursed his lips and nodded. "Something tells me, you're feeling a little bitter."

"You could say," I replied tersely.

I sat tight-lipped as Amy explained to Tom about her ever-increasing first-hand knowledge of the tourist spots of the world, courtesy of her parents' in-fighting. Tom listened patiently as I turned more and more green with envy.

She made a perfect take-off, as always, and expertly flew her private jet CHAS1, out of Rio de Janeiro. Garth, in the co-pilot's seat, leafed through a pile of holiday brochures.

"Where should we go next, darling?" He turned a page. "Water-skiing in Bermuda?"

"Been there."

"Shark fishing in the Caribbean?"

"Done that."

"Surfing in Hawaii?"

"Got the grass skirt."

"Have you seen the Pyramids? Victoria Falls? Taj Mahal? Great Barrier Reef?"

"Yep, yep, yep and yep."

Garth shrugged helplessly. "Then that's it, sweetie. You've been everywhere, done everything..."

"So you're not doing anything then at half-term?" Tom said, addressing me.

"I thought I just said that, dimbo. Weren't you listening?" I snapped back, which was a bit cheeky as I'd just spent the last few moments in my own dreamworld. Luckily neither Tom nor Amy commented on the fact.

"Just confirming," and he left with a strange look and, if I wasn't mistaken, a glint in his eye.

After half an hour Ms Hillier called a halt to the rehearsal and told us to gather on the stage where she proceeded to tell us that she expected us to have learned all our lines over half-term (I'd already learned mine in half a minute).

"No scripts after half-term. That means you as well, Deborah and Garth. I know you've got the most lines to learn, but you need to set an example to the others."

"No problem," replied Garth. Deborah just smiled.

"I also hope that many of you will be able to get together over the half-term and rehearse some of your scenes together."

I glared at Amy. She just shrugged.

"Especially you and Garth, Deborah," Ms Hillier continued. "You really do need to work on some of those scenes."

Just as I was about to explode with jealousy, Deborah put up her hand. "Sorry Ms Hiller, I can't. I'm going away for half-term," she simpered. "To the Maldives. They're a group of tropical islands in the Indian Ocean..."

There was a pause before Ms Hillier replied in a how-on-earth-do-these-parents-afford-these-holidays-I-bet-they're-not-teachers sort of voice. "Yes, I am aware of their location, Deborah."

Deborah continued in her annoying vein. "I thought a sun tan might help my interpretation of the role."

Ms Hillier (and the rest of the cast) looked bemused.

"It'll make me look more Italian!" explained the bubble-head. "Juliet *is* Italian, isn't she?"

Ms Hillier looked heavenwards. "Yes, she is Italian. So...?"

"So I thought a sun tan would make me more look more like an authentic Italian."

Ms Hillier obviously couldn't be bothered to explore Deborah's role preparations any longer and sent us off with a loud "Go! Everyone! And learn your lines!"

"I *do* hope Deborah doesn't catch any fatal diseases in the Maldives," I growled to Amy as we wandered off. "Just something nasty like dysentery or malaria."

That night as I lay reading *Romeo and Juliet* for the hundreth time, an idea popped into my head that was so brilliant that I shouted out in joy and hugged my duvet, my pillow and my teddy bear.

Because Deborah was away and couldn't help Garth go through his scenes, a substitute was needed. Me! I'd volunteer to go through Garth's scenes with him.

I giggled as I began to plan my capture. I'd get him round here when the house was clear, dazzle him with my charm, pick a good scene to rehearse and then...

Garth moved his lips closer to hers. "Darling," he whispered, "I've waited so long, for this moment.
His lips met hers as time stopped...

"Switch your light off Charlie. You've been reading for hours!"

Thanks Dad I thought, just when I was in the middle of a good dream!

"Get to sleep," he yelled.

This was easier to say than do. I didn't sleep much that night and I was at school first thing. I'd decided not to tell Amy my plan, just in case it all went horribly wrong. At break-time instead of going to the form room, I told her

I had to see Ms Hillier about rehearsal times and shot off towards the sixth-form common-room.

I stood outside summoning up the courage to put my head round the door. I didn't need to. Just as I was about to take the big step, Garth walked out.

My heart was thumping so loudly I was sure he'd hear it. It was like a steel band was playing inside my chest. I tried my best to be cool and nonchalant. "Oh Garth hi!"

Garth stopped and looked at me in a quizzical do-I-know-you? way.

"I'm Charlie. I'm in the play. Peter." He still didn't know. The steel band was now in full calypso mode. I took a deep breath and blurted out. "I bumped into you in the corridor and you fainted when you saw me bleeding." (Thanks a lot mouth! What a great line - he'll be dead impressed with being reminded of that, I thought.)

Light dawned. "Oh yeah. Charlie. Hi."

And in the next few minutes, whilst the steel band beat out a whole Caribbean medley, I volunteered my services to help him rehearse his scenes during half-term.

He listened, and then after a thousand-year pause, he said the words that I'd been waiting to hear.

"Yeah, OK. Thanks."

Cathedral bells rang the breadth and length of the country; thousands of doves were released and flew heavenwards; fireworks lit up the sky; rose petals swirled in the breeze and millions of people roared their approval.

"HE SAID 'YES'!!! THANK YOU! THANK YOU! THANK YOU!"

"How about Monday evening at my place?" I

suggested tentatively (thinking that if Monday night went well, we could spend the rest of the week 'rehearsing').

He nodded again. "Yeah. Great."

Cannons roared, drums boomed, waves crashed...

After I'd told Garth my address and set the time (*and* swapped mobile numbers – "just in case I needed to contact him", I'd innocently explained!) I turned and floated down the corridor on cloud nine-hundred and ninety-nine, with a grin as wide as it could go without splitting my face in two.

"Why have you got that grin on your face?" Tom stepped in front of me, bringing me momentarily down to cloud nine-hundred and ninety-eight.

"Because it would look silly on your face," I replied, wittily.

Surprisingly, Tom didn't make any sort of nasty comment back. Instead he burst out laughing. "Good one. Excellent." Then he paused and took a deep breath. "Er... Charlie, you um... you know erm... last night you er... said that er... you um... weren't er... doing anything over erm... half-term?"

I eyed him suspiciously. What was wrong? Tom didn't usually um and er as much as this.

"Well...er... neither am I... and... erm... I... er... wondered...er... I wondered... ifyoufancygoingtothecinema-withmeonsayMondaynight?"

It took me a few moments to decipher what Tom had said. Then it clicked. Garth was coming to learn lines on Monday night. Tom was asking me to go to the cinema on G-Day! I panicked. "I can't. I've... er... I've erm... (I was beginning to sound like Tom!) "... I've got to babysit. Nick. On Monday. And Tuesday and Wednesday and Thursday and Friday and the weekend. In fact every day and every night. All week. Sorry."

Tom shook his head. "That's okay. I was just wondering, because you'd said... you know. Well, maybe next half-term, or Christmas..." He turned and shot off.

"Boys," I thought as I watched Tom go. "Strange things." I turned down the corridor, floated back up a cloud and skipped to my next lesson. People stared at me, but I didn't care. Monday was G-Day!

ACT 3, SCENE 2

At my poor house, look to behold this night
Earth-treading stars that make dark heaven light.
(Romeo and Juliet, **I. ii**)

Mum came into the sitting-room and stopped, rigid with shock. She staggered backwards, theatrically clutching her forehead.

"I don't believe it!" she gasped. "It cannot be! Is't possible that I should live to see this sight?"

I put some more polish on the coffee table. "Ha, ha, very funny."

"I must be hallucinating." She picked up the phone. "Hello, is that the psychiatric unit? You've got to help me, I thought I just saw my daughter doing the housework."

"Sarcasm is the lowest form of wit," I told her.

She put the phone down. "They said they couldn't

help me, but I should ring the *Guinness Book of World Records*." She sat down. "What's the occasion?"

I clicked my tongue crossly. "I've just hoovered that chair!"

"Dearie me, it must be royalty at least."

"If you must know, I've got a friend coming round. I'm helping him to learn his lines."

"Oh, really?" Her eyes narrowed and I knew I was in for at least ten minutes of the who-is-he-do-I-know-him-do-I-know-his-parents-is-he-wanted-by-the-police? treatment, but at that moment the phone rang. Mum answered it while I dusted the fireplace.

"Oh, hello, Mrs Morris. Nick's just getting ready... (Long pause)...oh dear... Yes... Well, of course not... Yes, I see... Of course you don't... No, we'll be fine..."

At this point I began to get a very bad feeling about this call. Phil Morris was the mate Nick was supposed to be staying with tonight.

"... Don't worry... I hope he's feeling better soon... yes, well, thanks for ringing... yes... goodbye..."

She put the phone down. "That was Phil's mum. The poor little devil's just come down with chickenpox. I'm afraid you'll have to look after Nick this evening..."

I twisted the duster between nerveless fingers. "No, it can't be... tell me it isn't true..."

Mum sighed heavily. "Now don't you start being difficult..."

"Difficult?!" How could I explain to her how important this was? "Can't he go and stay with Martin? Or Richard?" I was practically babbling by now. "Can't he go to Gran's? Or Aunty Irene's? What about putting him up for adoption?"

"Don't be silly." Mum stood up and put on her Firm but Fair voice as recommended in her *Good Parenting Handbook*. "I'm sorry, Charlie, but your father's away on a residential course and I've got a committee meeting. I don't suppose for a minute Nick will make a nuisance of himself."

I didn't suppose it for a minute, either; I supposed it for several hours, until I managed to get Nick on his own and had a word with him.

I told him that I had arranged for Garth to come round so that I could help him with his lines. Before he'd even managed to get the leer arranged on his face, I gave my dear little brother to understand that if he annoyed Garth, embarrassed me, or generally messed about in any way at all, I would personally give him a whole-body rubdown with a cheese grater. "And that will just be for starters," I told him. "What you're going to do is, you're going to go to your room and stay there. You're going to play your computer games very quietly, and you are not going to come downstairs for a biscuit, or a drink of water, or because you thought you heard a noise, or for any other reason whatever; because if you do, I shall nail you to the shed door and whip you to death with barbed-wire."

Mum went out at six and I shooed the Swamp Thing upstairs. He had a nasty sly look on his face that I didn't like one bit, but I couldn't think of anything else to threaten him with; I just hoped he'd take the hint.

I opened my wardrobe door and stood there deciding what to wear.

She lounged exquisitely on the priceless Chippendale sofa. Garth sat, calm and amused, beside her, dressed immaculately in a suit of his own design.

Marcel, the greatest living Paris fashion designer knelt on the white lambs-wool rug at her feet. Tears streamed down his face. "Sharlee, CHERIE, do not break my 'eart! You must model only POUR MOI!"

"Sorry, MON AMI," she drawled, crossing her legs (insured for ten million dollars) with a rustle of silk. "I'm under exclusive contract to the House of Garth."

Marcel rose, gathering the tattered shreds of his dignity. "Zen I 'ave nossing left to live for. ADIEU, CHERIE."

Charlie barely noticed as the desperate couturier hurled himself through the nineteenth-storey window of her office; she and Garth were too busy planning an empire that would change the fashion world forever...

Actually, looking through my wardrobe, I reckoned that one of those hermits who live on top of a pole probably had more choice of what to wear than I did. By the time I'd dismissed everything that was too scruffy, as well as everything that was too tarty (I didn't want Garth to run away screaming as soon as I opened the door) I was down to my white jeans, and a choice between my maroon silk shirt and my cream and brown sweater. I laid them out on the bed while I went and:

1) had a shower;

2) brushed my teeth until my gums bled;

3) gargled a whole bottle of mouth wash (which I'd managed to get Mum to buy by pretending I'd got a mouth ulcer);

4) sprayed my mouth with *Fresh Breff* (for guaranteed *Fresh Breff* confidence twenty-four hours a day);

5) brushed my teeth again.

While I was in the bathroom, the cat came in and lay down on the shirt, so that settled what I was going to wear.

I drenched myself with that scent that makes men drop whatever they're doing and buy expensive bunches of flowers for perfect strangers, and made a mental note to demand my money back if I didn't end up fighting Garth off with the poker. Then I went downstairs.

Plate of cheesy nibbles on coffee table – check;

Sophisticated magazine casually spread half-open on sofa – check;

Hearth-rug covering wine stain on carpet – check;

Coffee machine primed and ready to go – check;

Selection of music to smooch by, for later (please God!) - check.

The door bell rang.

Right, I told myself. Stay calm. He's just coming round to learn lines. There's no need for panic. Be cool, suave, sophisticated. I opened the door.

He was standing there. On the doorstep. He himself. Garth. On my doorstep. Standing.

Manfully he swept her into a passionate embrace. She felt the passionate thudding of his heart, pounding restlessly against his ribs. Their gazes locked. Time stood still. Their mouths met in an endless kiss...

"Hi!" I squeaked.

I showed him into the spotless (for once) sitting-room. "You'll have to excuse the mess," I gushed, plumping up a cushion. I daresay I was fluttering my eyelashes at him. Come on, girl, I thought furiously, get a grip.

I took a deep breath. "Won't you take a seat?" I asked in something like a normal voice. He smiled and moved to a chair. I felt a great wave of relief wash over me. It was going to be all right.

Garth sat down.

"FFFTTTHHHWWWAAAAARRRRRRRRPPPPP!"

Garth shot up again like a startled deer. I gazed at him in total horror. With one eye on me, he reached under the chair seat and pulled out a whoopee cushion.

"Ah," he said, "yes. Very funny."

I opened and shut my mouth like a goldfish. "It's not mine," I managed to blurt at last. "Nick must have put it there. Sorry!" I took the dreadful limp thing from him and threw it behind the sofa. "Nick, my little brother. You know what little brothers are like. Ahahaha."

"Ahahaha." Garth sat down, more carefully this time.

"Coffee?" I said brightly.

"Er, yes..." He sounded a bit nervous.

I went into the kitchen and switched on the machine. Should I kill Nick now or later? I decided later. I didn't want any tell-tale blood dripping down through the ceiling.

I went back to Garth, who seemed to have calmed down a bit. "Shall we start with the party scene?" I asked.

"Sorry?"

I picked up the book and handed it to him. "The Capulets' party. Act one, scene five."

"Oh, yes, all right." He turned to the scene "You follow the lines and stop me if I go wrong." He handed the book back to me. "OK?"

"OK," I breathed.

He closed his eyes and began:

"If I profane with my unworthiest hand
This holy shrine, the gentle sin is this..."

76

"Um..." I said.

He opened his eyes. "That was right, wasn't it?"

"Oh, yes... but when Romeo talks about profaning a holy shrine, isn't he supposed to hold Juliet's hand?"

"Well, yes, but we're only doing lines..."

"I just thought it might help you get the feeling of the line. If we did it properly. You know."

He gave me an uncertain look. "The feeling of the line. Erm... OK, fine." He took my hand.

"If I profane with my unworthiest hand
This holy shrine, the gentle sin is this.
My lips, two blushing pilgrims, ready stand
To smooth that rough touch..."

Hardly breathing, I leaned towards him. He hesitated, then went on,

"To smooth that rough touch with a tender kiss..."

Slowly, he tilted his head and inched closer to me....

There was a tapping from the window. I glanced over Garth's shoulder... and let rip an ear-piercing scream.

Garth scrambled back across the sofa. "Who?... What?... Where?..." he gabbled. I pointed at the window and screamed again at the terrifying spider, as big as a man's hand, crawling up the glass. Suddenly it jerked straight upwards, out of sight. By the time Garth turned to face the window, there was nothing there.

He looked back at me. "What's the matter?" He sounded pretty rattled. I couldn't blame him.

"It was... I thought I saw... Out there... I could have

sworn I..."

I took a deep breath. It was Nick, of course. He had a collection of horrible plastic creepy crawlies, and he'd obviously dangled one down on a piece of cotton or something and swung it against the window to make the tapping noise and then jiggled it about to make it look alive. But there was no point in telling Garth that. Trying to explain would only make matters worse.

I drew the curtains. "I'm sorry. I thought I saw something... horrible... on the window, but it's not there now."

He was staring at me. "Something horrible."

"Er... yes."

"On the window."

"That's it," I said brightly.

"But it's not there now."

"Um... right."

"I see."

He was breathing pretty heavily, but I didn't think that passionate feelings for me were uppermost in his mind just at the moment.

"I'll go and see if the coffee's ready, shall I?" I gave him a brittle smile and legged it for the kitchen.

I would *shred* Nick for this. I would batter him until he was no more than a smear on the walls. I would...

I forced myself to calm down. Forget Nick. He was for later. Right now I had to sort things out with Garth, I would explain, that's what I'd do. Explain. He'd understand that I couldn't help having a little brother who was the spawn of Satan. It could happen to anyone. I'd explain about the plastic spider. Over coffee. That was it. I'd take the coffee in, and we'd drink it, and calm down, and I'd explain everything, and in five minutes we'd both be laughing...

I took the coffee in. Garth was standing by the door looking ready to bolt through it if I showed any more signs of craziness. I gave him a reassuring smile and a mug with happy bunnies on it.

"Um... thanks," he said.

"Sugar?"

"Two, please."

I poured two heaped teaspoons full of sugar into his coffee, and stirred. He almost smiled. "I think I need this."

I gave a tinkling laugh and took a drink from my mug. It wasn't that warm by now. Garth took a generous swig of his coffee...

... his eyes widened in shock...

... and he doubled up, explosively spitting out his coffee. It settled across the carpet in a brown mist.

I stared at him in astonishment. Didn't he like the brand?

He turned and gazed at me with goggling eyes. "Salt..." he managed to gasp, "you put... salt... in my... oh, God!"

He bolted through the door. I heard the front door fling open, and a moment later the sound of Garth being very ill into the azaleas.

Feeling as if I was in a nightmare and couldn't wake up, I moistened my little finger, and dipped it into the white crystals in the sugar bowl. I touched them to my tongue. It was salt, all right. Somebody had put salt in the sugar bowl, and it didn't take Sherlock Holmes to work out who.

I dashed to the front door. Garth appeared in the light of a streetlamp, walking very quickly away down the street with a handkerchief to his mouth. For a moment I considered chasing after him and trying to explain, but I didn't think he'd be in any mood to listen. I'd have to try and sort it out later.

I heard the back door slam. I sprinted upstairs. Nick's room was empty. From the bedroom window I could see the back reflector of his bike as he pedalled down the path at the back of the house. He was going as if the hounds of hell were after him. They weren't, but something worse was. Me.

Nick could run, but he couldn't hide. I could wait.

My little brother was dead meat.

Act 3, Scene 3

I will withdraw. But this intrusion shall,
Now seeming sweet, convert to bitterest gall.
(Romeo and Juliet, I. v)

Nick didn't come home until after Mum had got back from her council meeting. He came in right behind her, and got a good earbashing for his trouble.

"Where have you been? You know we don't like you being out after dark, especially not on your bike, it hasn't got proper lights or anything." Mum turned to me. "What were you doing letting Nick go out?"

I told her that I hadn't 'let' Nick go out, he'd nipped out of the back door while I was seeing Garth off at the front. I didn't mention the salt in the sugar bowl or the fact that my date with Garth had been ruined by Nick. I didn't want Mum to know that I had changed my plans for the next few days. The list of Things to Do in my diary now included, 'Get even with my little brother'.

If Mum knew what was in my mind, I'd have to listen to a lot of speeches about how Every Argument Can Be Resolved If Only People Act Reasonably, and Violence Never Solves Anything, and I'd have to promise to sort out my differences with Nick in Frank and Friendly Discussions instead of, for example, Roasting Him Over A Slow Fire or Gutting Him with a Blunt Bread Knife. On the other hand, I wanted Nick to know exactly what I had in mind. I wanted him to suffer. So all the time Mum was telling him off, I stood behind her making throat-cutting signs and mouthing the words, "You're dead!" He tried to keep the usual aggravating smirk on his face, but his eyes kept darting about from me to the stairs. He looked as if he was weighing up whether he could get to his room before I got to him.

Eventually, Mum ran out of steam and sent Nick to bed. I waited for a bit, then did a lot of yawning and said I was going to bed, too. Mum gave me a funny look and asked me if I was ill.

"No," I said, "why do you ask?"

"It's just that it usually takes a fifteen-minute argument to persuade you to go to bed at a reasonable time. I don't think I could get you to go to bed early at gunpoint."

"I'm just tired, okay?" I gave another jaw-breaking yawn to prove the point, then dragged myself wearily out of the sitting room. Once I was out of Mum's sight, I went up the stairs three at a time and slid into Nick's room.

He was sitting bolt upright in bed. "If you belt me, I'll tell mum," he quavered.

I stood over him. I looked at him as if he was half a caterpillar I'd just found in my lettuce.

"You're a horrible, stupid little sprog," I told him,

very quietly. "I hate you. I hate your stupid face and your stupid jokes and your stupid grin. I hate it when people know you're my brother." I felt my fists begin to clench. "How do you think I feel having a brother like you?"

Nick turned on me like a cornered rat. "Well, how do you think I feel having a sister like you?" he whined, "who keeps going off into daydreams and standing there looking at nothing until everybody thinks you're *mental?*"

"Oh yes?" I snarled. "What about you? You want to talk about mental? What about last year when you got an old curtain out of the dressing-up box and wore it like a cloak, and put your underpants on over your trousers and went rushing round outside yelling you were Captain Cosmos and shooting foam rubber pellets at people?"

"That was just a game."

"I'll never live it down. You are so *embarrassing.* All my friends think you're weird..."

"Well, all *my* friends think *you're* weird!"

I stood up. "I'm not going to argue with you. I can't stand the sight of you. You make me sick. You've just messed up my big chance of going out with Garth."

"I did what you told me!" said Nick triumphantly. "You said don't come down while Garth was there, and I didn't."

I grabbed him by the shoulders and squeezed hard. "Listen, you little pile of snot, I'm not playing games. I'm going to make you pay for tonight. I'm not going to tell you what I'm going to do, and I'm not going to tell you when I'm going to do it. It could be tomorrow, it could be next week or next month, but it's going to happen, and when it does you are going to be very, very sorry you messed with me." I went to the door and turned the light off. "Sleep tight."

I'd already decided what I was going to do to Nick, but I needed the house to myself for a few hours. It didn't matter, I could wait; and in the meantime, every time I saw Nick looking at me, I shot him with my fingers, just to let him know I hadn't forgotten. The longer I waited, the more he'd suffer.

The stranger wore a battered hat and a poncho, and rode a mule.

Curious eyes watched from behind shuttered windows as the oddly dressed figure hitched the sweating mount to the post outside the livery stable, then strolled across to the saloon.

The barkeeper polished the stained wooden counter. "You lookin' for someone, maybe?"

The stranger took in the saloon with hooded eyes. "Tell Mexican Nick I want to see him."

A voice from behind the stranger said, "Who ees looking for Mexican Neek?"

The stranger turned slowly. "Who wants to know?"

Mexican Nick sneered. He held two six shooters pointing unwaveringly at the stranger. "You talk preety beeg for a dead man."

The stranger fixed the outlaw with a steely gaze. "I bin lookin' for you a long time, Nick. Mighty long time."

Mexican Nick spat on the floor. "Bounty hunter, eh? Peoples like you come after Mexican Neek before."

The stranger lit a cheroot. "Not exactly like me, Nick."

The first bullet plugged the barrel of Nick's right hand gun. The second bullet plugged the barrel of the left. Both guns exploded in Nick's hands.

"They call me Catch-up Charlie," growled the stranger, pulling the hat from her head. Long hair tumbled to her shoulders. "You bin a bad boy, Nick. Now, you're gonna pay."

Aiming for a spot dead in the centre of the quivering bandit's forehead, she pulled the trigger...

I tried to phone Garth every day of the holiday, but all I got was his voicemail. I didn't dare leave a message. I would just have to try and explain when we got back to school. Apart from that, all I did was hang out round the shopping centre to see if there was anyone about. There wasn't. I thought about ringing or texting Tom, but I'd told him I was busy and I didn't want to have to get into any complicated explanations of why I suddenly wasn't. What a great holiday! Thank you, Nick!

Dad came home at the weekend. On Sunday, he decided to drag us all out for a walk so we could all get, as he put it, a good clean dose of healthy country air (though why air that smells of concentrated pig-muck is supposed to be good for you, don't ask me). Perfect! I told Dad I had a headache. I don't think he believed me, but I heard him say to Mum that at least they'd be able to enjoy a walk without me and Nick sniping at each other all the way round, and he didn't push it.

So off they went, and I got busy. There was a lot to do, but I had no interruptions. By the time they came back, my revenge on Nick was complete and the best part was, he didn't even know it had happened.

Yet.

On Monday I arrived at school just in time to see Garth and Deborah greeting each other like long lost twins (though with a lot more kissing and cuddling than you'd expect from twins, no matter how long they'd been lost). I heard Garth tell Deborah how amazing her tan was; she said something I didn't catch about "white bits". Then she saw me looking at them and gave me one of her very sweetest smiles, while Garth gave me a look that was about as warm as the seat in an Eskimo's outside loo.

The whole day passed in a haze of misery. Tom was still mad at me for not going out with him, and Amy was too full of her holiday to want to listen to me moaning. I had nothing to look forward to but home time. But I was looking forward to that quite a lot.

I made sure I got home before Nick and was stretched out on the sofa reading a mag when he shambled in.

"My day for the TV," he said, expecting an argument. Usually he'd have got one, but today I just shrugged. He gave me a suspicious glare, then went to get one of his favourite *Captain Cosmos* DVDs. He pushed it into the machine, and pressed the 'play' button.

The screen filled with 'snow', and a hissing sound came from the speaker. There was no picture.

Nick looked puzzled. He ejected the DVD and wiped it on his jumper. He put it back in the machine and pressed 'play' again.

There was still no picture.

"Stupid thing! What's wrong with it?"

He selected another DVD, put it in the machine and pressed 'play'.

Nothing.

I watched Nick tense up as a horrible suspicion crossed his mind. "Have you done something to this?"

I gave him a crocodile grin. "It's amazing what happens to DVDs when you put them in a microwave and switch it on... The sparking and flashes of electricity are quite incredible. I learnt all about it in science…"

Nick looked from me to the snow-filled screen and back again. His eyes grew round with horror. "All of them?" he said in a strangled whisper.

"Yup."

"You can't have!" Nick screeched. "It took me ages to find them. I had the complete set! Even the special Japanese imports! I'll never be able to get any more copies! They cost a fortune… and you put them in the microwave?!"

I nodded. "Two minutes at full power… They're certainly cooked. Captain Cosmos has met his match! Not so indestructible!"

Nick gave a howl and threw himself on me, fists flailing; but I was still stronger than him, and held him off until he caught me a crack round the ear, so I thumped him back. He rolled on the carpet sobbing. "Cow! Rotten, filthy cow!"

I gave him a contemptuous look. "Crybaby."

He blundered out of the room. I heard him slam out of the kitchen and drag the garage door open. A few seconds later I heard the rattling of his bike as he shot down the path.

Then I heard a screech of brakes, and a crunch.

All the next bit was like a horrible dream.

I rushed out of the house. There was a car slewed round in the road. Nick's bike was a tangled wreck lying underneath it.

Nick was lying in the road in front of the car. He was very still and his head was bleeding. The driver was getting out of the car. He kept saying over and over again, "He just shot out in front of me. There was nothing I could do."

Another car stopped. The driver got out and started talking into a mobile phone. I found myself kneeling by

Nick, calling his name. I reached out to touch him, but Mrs Patterson from across the street was there and she said I shouldn't move Nick, there was an ambulance coming. "Shall I phone your mum?" she asked. I said I'd do it.

Then I was in the hall, holding the phone, listening to the ringing tone.

"Hello, can I speak to Mrs Robbins please?"

"I'm afraid she's in a staff meeting at the moment..."

I gripped the phone tighter. "Would you ask her to come to the phone please? I'm her daughter. It's urgent."

A few moments later, Mum was on the line. "Charlie? What's wrong?"

"Nick's had an accident, Mum. Can you come home, please?"

"What's happened?"

"He was on his bike. A car hit him."

A heard her catch her breath. "Is he alright?"

My voice broke. "I don't know, Mum."

"Phone your dad."

She rang off. I phoned Dad's office. He wasn't there, so I rang his mobile. That wasn't switched on, so I left a gabbled, tearful message on his voicemail and rang off.

Then the ambulance arrived. The ambulance men put Nick on a stretcher. Mrs Patterson said she'd tell Mum and Dad where we were and look after the house. A policeman was talking to the driver whose car had hit Nick. He was still saying, "There was nothing I could do," when the ambulance doors closed.

At the hospital, they wheeled Nick off for an X-ray and told me to wait. Mum came in. She was trying very hard to be calm. She asked me what happened. I told her about the accident. I started to cry; I couldn't stop. Mum hugged me, and the worst thing of all was that I kept thinking that when she found out what I'd done, she'd never want to hug me again.

Then Dad arrived. I had to explain what had happened all over again while Mum went off with a nurse to see what was happening to Nick.

After what seemed a long time, mum came back with a lady doctor.

"He's a lucky boy," she said briskly. "A few cuts and bruises, a spot of gravel rash; he's had a nasty crack on the head though. We'd like to keep him in overnight for observation, in case of concussion." Mum made a funny little noise in her throat and hugged me so hard I thought my bones would break.

Dad stayed at the hospital while Mum took me home. She made us a cup of tea. We sat down at the kitchen table. Then she said, "All right, Charlie, what happened?"

"I told you about the accident."

"But you haven't told me why it happened. Nick's normally very careful on his bike. What happened between you two to make him shoot off like that?"

I opened my mouth to deny everything and then shut it. I felt my eyes fill with tears again; then I sat at the kitchen table, put my head on my arms and burst into sobs.

When I could speak, I told Mum everything; about the whoopee cushion, and the spider, and the salt, and what I done to Nick's DVDs. It all came pouring out in waves of guilt, like being sick with words. The whole story sounded worse when I started to tell it. I felt almost like another person, listening to a mean, spiteful version of myself explaining what had happened to an accompaniment of sniffs.

When I'd finished, Mum stared at me and said, quite gently, "Charlie, he's your *brother*."

"What about what he did to me?"

"Charlie, for God's sake, he's *eleven years old*." Mum pushed her hair back from her face. She looked tired.

Dad came home. He said Nick was asleep and the hospital would ring in the morning to let us know when we could come and collect him. Mum told Dad what had happened and he looked at me as if I was a stranger. It was worse than if he's shouted the place down. He told me to go to bed. I went upstairs and lay on my bed fully dressed and stared at the ceiling.

Nick was going to be all right.

The shouting would start tomorrow.

ACT 4

Act 4, Scene 1

Oh serpent heart, hid with a flowering face!
(Romeo and Juliet, III .ii)

"Not a chance!" Mum folded her arms. "You're still grounded, in case you'd forgotten."

I stared at her. "But Amy arranged this sleepover before half-term, and you said I could go."

"That was then. This is now."

"I don't believe this! I've said I'm sorry, I've offered to buy Nick some more rotten DVDs, are you going to punish me for the rest of my life?"

Nick had been sent home the morning after the accident with a bandage round his head that he reckoned made him look like Rambo. His cool-rating had gone up about five hundred percent when he showed it off at school. He was getting a new bike on the insurance. I'd practically done him a favour, but I'd not been allowed out ever since the accident, except I was allowed to go to rehearsals and be ignored by Garth, big deal. I had the social life of a mushroom. There was nothing for me to do except learn Juliet's lines; by now, I knew them backwards.

I tried to reason with Mum. "But it's Friday night..."

"No."

I lost my temper. "It's so unfair. You're always taking Nick's side. It's not me who can't ride a bike without looking where he's going..."

"I don't want to hear another word!"...

...the Chief Warder roared, spittle flying from her snarling lips. "There is no escape from Alcatraz!"

She twisted her lips into a bitter smile. "Tell it to the marines, warder. The prison ain't been built that could hold Mad Dog Charlie."

The Chief Warder's sadistic features turned purple with fury. "Is zat so?" she snarled.

The Con Queen laughed in her face. "Save ya breath, screw. I'm outta here, tonight!"

I waited for fifteen minutes after I heard Mum and Dad go to bed before I got up. I'd put my nightshirt on over my T-shirt and jeans in case Mum came in to give me a few more Sorrowful Looks before bedtime, but she was playing the let's-just-ignore-her-and-see-how-she-likes-it game instead, so I needn't have bothered. I took my nightshirt off and stuffed it in my rucksack, along with some DVDs, a couple of books and a hairbrush. Then I bundled my duvet up as small as it would go and opened the bedroom door very quietly.

The latch on the front door made a click like a gunshot. I held my breath and waited. Nothing happened.

I slipped through and pulled the door closed behind me. This time the click of the latch sounded like somebody dropping a tin bath on a tiled floor, and I didn't wait to find out if anyone had heard. I legged it, with my duvet unrolling and tripping me up.

When I got to Amy's, everyone else had already arrived. They were all drinking something pink that Amy had sloshed up in her mum's biggest mixing bowl. "It's punch," Mary told me as she handed me some in a teacup. "It's got a whole bottle of vodka in it." She wandered off, swaying a bit and giggling.

I sniffed it suspiciously. "Has this really got a whole bottle of vodka in it?" I asked Amy.

Amy gave me a wink and lifted the flap of the rubbish bin. Lying on top there was one of those little miniature sample bottles they sell on trains. "A whole bottle," she whispered, tapping the side of her nose.

I stared at it. "Well, nobody's going to get very drunk on that."

"You'd be surprised." Amy led me into the sitting room. It was lit only by a few candles. I peered into the gloom. Besides Mary, Lisa was there, and Sandra, and half a dozen others. They were all being very loud and rolling about giggling like anything. A few people were dancing to the music from Amy's stereo, and bumping into things.

Everyone was in a nightshirt or pyjamas or whatever, so I nipped upstairs to put mine on. When I came down, they'd turned the music off and put a DVD on. "What are we watching?" I asked.

There was a chorus of "shussshes" and Amy beckoned me to sit next to her on the floor. "*Nightmare Of The Flesh-eating Zombies, Part Six*," she whispered. "This is the opening bit, where Eloise gets her head pulled off. Watch."

Well, I did, but several gallons of blood later I was feeling a bit ill. As each victim died horribly, everybody cheered and shouted funny comments. I turned to look at Amy...

Charlie smiled pityingly. "Oh, gee, Amy Lou, honey, what in tarnation are you so skeered of? Just a'cause there's a maniac on the loose murderin' folks in unspeakably gruesome ways don't mean we shouldn't go to the high school prom... Amy Lou?..." She touched her friend on the shoulder. Amy Lou's head suddenly tilted back at an impossible angle. Her throat had been cut from ear to ear.

As she stifled a scream of terror, Charlie heard the sound of heavy breathing from the darkness behind her; out of the corner of her eye, she caught a glimpse of shining metal...

I gave a squeak and put my head under my duvet. When the music had finished going *SCREEEINK SCREEEINK SCREEEINK* and I thought it was safe to come out, I nipped behind the sofa with a candle and read my book, trying to ignore the screams and sloshing noises from the TV.

Half a dozen grisly slayings later, there was a ring at the doorbell. Amy went to get it. There was a shriek of laughter from the hall. I stuck my head round the side of the sofa to see who had come in. The sitting-room door flung open, and Deborah swept through.

For a second, I didn't recognise her. She was dressed to kill. Her clothes were outrageous; the sort of catwalk creations that fashion designers insist will take the high street by storm but never do. Her make up was a tracery of black lines on a deathly-pale foundation, with purple eye sockets and a blood red mouth that made her face look like a moth's wings. She waved a bottle in the air and brayed with laughter again like a demented donkey. "Lisa, darling!" she screeched and gave her a big hug.

There was a moment's silence, then everyone was around Deborah, hugging and kissing and trying hard not to be out-shrieked by anyone else. Someone switched the DVD off. Amy stood in the doorway with her mouth open. She caught my eye and shrugged.

"I've just been out with Garth," confided Deborah in

a voice you could have heard in Aberdeen. "He's an absolute ANIMAL! He bit me, LOOK!" She tilted her chin to show off a bit of purple skin just above her collarbone.

I gritted my teeth. Ever since half-term, Deborah and Garth had been An Item. She never lost the chance to remind people of this, especially if I was around. During rehearsals, they were always somewhere at the back of the hall trying to swallow each other while I sat there trying to concentrate on the play and being eaten alive by jealousy.

"Where's the booze then? What's this?" Deborah took a suspicious sniff of Amy's punch. "Boooooring - Ribena and cough medicine! How about we pep it up a bit?" She waved her bottle again. It was Bacardi.

She swept Amy aside and headed for the kitchen, with the rest of the girls in tow, teacups at the ready. Amy scampered over and knelt on the carpet beside me. "Charlie, we've got to stop her!"

I shrugged. "How?"

Amy's shoulders slumped. There wasn't any way of breaking up the party that wouldn't have left her with the street cred of a quilted anorak. She gave me a pleading look. "Help me!"

At about four in the morning Amy and I were sitting in the bathroom. Most of the others were asleep. Deborah had taken over the party. She'd held court, told a string of blood-curdlingly filthy jokes, sloshed booze around, screeched at everything anyone said to her and had not been struck by lightning, though I asked God to do it any number of times. She'd still been going strong when she'd left at half-past three. By that time, Amy's house was wrecked; and so were most of her guests.

Lisa had been sick once. Sandra had been sick twice. Mary had just passed out. Amy's sitting room looked as if a troop of baboons had been playing basketball all over it. She sat on the edge of the bath, wringing her hands.

"I mean, Deborah!" she moaned. "Miss Goody Two-Shoes, Butter Wouldn't Melt In My Knickers! Did you see her? That make up! That hair! Those nails!" (Did I mention the nails? Black, if anyone's interested.)

"Garth obviously didn't mind," I said bitterly.

Amy gave me a slantwise look. "Well, he bit her," she said primly, "that can't have been very nice."

I stared at her. "Are you kidding?"

"You wouldn't mind if he bit you?"

"I wouldn't mind if he ate me."

"Anyway, we've only got her word for it that it WAS Garth. She probably did it herself with the vacuum cleaner." Amy put her head in her hands. "Mum'll be back this afternoon. I'll never get this mess cleaned up!"

I sighed. "Not sitting here, we won't, anyway. Come on."

For the next couple of hours we cleared up the worst of the mess to a chorus of snores.

At half-past six, I said, "I've got to go. Mum and Dad don't know I'm out, I've got to be back in bed before they get up."

"Okay." Amy gave my hand a squeeze. "Thanks for helping me clear up. You're a star."

When I got back home, I tiptoed round the side of the house and slipped my back-door key into the lock. It turned with a slight click; I twisted the door handle and pushed.

Nothing happened.

I pushed again. The door must be bolted - but Dad never bolted it unless we were going away and leaving the house empty. I began to panic. I pushed harder... and suddenly realised that there was someone standing behind me, breathing heavily.

I turned slowly. Behind me was a creature out of nightmares. Its lips were curled in a terrible sneer, its chin sprouted stubble: its hair was wild, its eyes sunken and bloodshot.

"Oh, hello, Dad," I quavered.

He was quivering with fury. "All night I've been waiting for you! All bloody night! I rang your mobile – no answer! Where have you been?"

He grabbed me by the arm and dragged me round to the front of the house and in through the front door. Then I got the third degree, big time.

What did I mean by staying out all night, at my age, after Mum had expressly told me I couldn't? Hadn't I given them enough grief over Nick? Mum had been worried sick, and he'd spent all night on the sofa listening for me to come in, did I realise that? I was an irresponsible idiot, I'd always been an irresponsible idiot but now I was an even bigger irresponsible idiot. Evidently the punishment they'd given me after Nick's accident hadn't been severe enough. And what on earth had I been up to anyway? Were there lads at this orgy I'd been to? Good God, I stank of booze... was I drunk as well?

I tried to explain about Deborah and that Lisa had spilled her drink on my duvet, but I might as well have tried to argue with an earthquake. I was a disobedient pain in the neck, and he washed his hands of me and he was stopping my allowance and grounding me until the next ice age.

He stopped yelling at me at last, and I escaped to my room for a bit of desperately needed zizz. A couple of hours later I was dragged out of bed by Mum, who'd decided to take me shopping with her as a punishment.

I stopped at the window of the least cool clothing store in town, to which Mum had insisted on dragging me. I stared at my reflection. A bleary-eyed wreck with a bird's-nest hairdo stared back at me.

"Cooee! Charlie!" Deborah sailed past on the opposite pavement with her Mum. She gave me a cheery wave. She looked bright eyed and squeaky clean, like a convent girl on her way to confirmation.

Act 4, Scene 2

Is there no pity sitting in the clouds
That sees into the bottom of my grief?
(Romeo and Juliet, Act III. V)

I'd just about recovered by Monday and at school during break-time, Amy and I were holding a post-sleepover inquest when Tom bounded over. "I heard you had an all female rave-up and some people weren't very well. And I've heard that *someone* got in major trouble when they got home," he said pointedly. "What happened?"

"Don't ask," I replied rolling my eyes heavenwards.

"Okay, I won't," shrugged Tom.

There was a silence as Tom sat swinging his legs, looking around the form room. I tutted and nudged Amy.

She nodded knowingly.

"Tom?" she asked. "Don't boys know *anything*?"

"Eh?" he grunted.

"Although Charlie said 'Don't ask', she doesn't mean 'Don't ask', what she means is '*Do* ask', even though she's saying 'Don't'. Understand?"

A cloud of confusion drifted across Tom's face. You could practically see the neurons in his brain flashing on and off as he considered the implications of what Amy had said. After a couple of seconds he pursed his lips, looked at me, looked at Amy, looked back at me and raised his eyebrows quizzically.

I nodded. Amy nodded. He nodded. I smiled. Amy smiled. He smiled. "It's a girl thing isn't it?"

I nodded again.

"Right. Sooooo...." he took a deep breath, "What happened on Friday night?"

"You don't want to know..."

"Yes I do!" he screamed in frustration. "When I say 'what happened on Friday night?' I *don't* mean 'Please don't tell me what happened on Friday night?' I mean 'Please tell me what happened on Friday night'! It's simple; it's obvious."

"It must be a boy thing." Amy ventured. I nodded in agreement.

"Right, forget it!" Tom jumped off the table. "I haven't got the time for this girl-boy psychology. I think I'll go to the library and read some books on advanced nuclear physics - it'll be a lot easier than trying to understand you two." He stormed out of the classroom. Amy and I watched him go and burst out laughing.

"So how was your Dad?" Amy enquired when we'd

finished giggling.

I looked her in the eye. "Don't ask!"

"What night do you want to go and see the play?" I asked Mum and Dad as we sat at the dinner table. I'd taken advantage of a rare opportunity when we were all together as a 'family' to peg them down to a night (although this amazing event was only going to last a few moments as Dad was due at a late evening lecture and Mum had a meeting to go to).

Dad looked up from reading some notes. "What play?" he mumbled.

"The play I've been rehearsing for the last three months," I snapped back. "*Romeo and Juliet*." I could see Mum shaking her head at Dad.

"Charlie has told you about it, haven't you love," Mum said, opening her eyes wide and pursing her lips at Dad.

Dad took the hint. "Oh right yes, *Romeo and Juliet*. Good. When's it on?"

"Next week," I said through gritted teeth. "Wednesday, Thursday, Friday."

Dad looked thoughtful. "Hmmm. Might be a problem. Why haven't you said something earlier?"

I felt my anger starting to bubble in my stomach. "I told Mum ages ago that she had to let me know what night she wanted tickets. Didn't I?" I turned to Mum and caught her mouthing the words "I forgot" to Dad. My anger began shooting towards my mouth. "Oh great. You forgot. Thanks."

"All right love, don't get angry," soothed Mum, "I'm

sure we can sort out a night when we can come and see it."

But they couldn't. Dad was in a meeting on Wednesday, but reckoned that he could make Thursday if he could get someone to cover his session on Stress and Time Management, but that was no good for Mum as she had a PTA meeting on Thursday and an evening class on Wednesday. They could both make Friday, but Nick couldn't because he was supposed to be going bowling with his mates. At that point Nick said that he wasn't going to see any boring Shakespeare play, especially with his dippy sister in it, at which following point, I grabbed him round the neck and had to be wrestled off him by Dad and then Mum shouted that we should just sit down, stop shouting, stop squabbling and start acting like a normal family. (Oh yeah, I thought. We're really normal.)

We sat around the table staring at each other and breathing hard. I was seething. My leg was shaking and I couldn't have clenched my fists any harder if I'd tried.

Dad looked around, coughed and said, "We have a problem. I'm sensing anger within the family."

Great Dad, I thought. Mr Perceptive.

He continued. "Maybe I should ring Jim up at the centre and arrange for us all to have a session of family therapy."

I couldn't believe it. "Why do we have to go to family therapy?" I howled.

"Because we've got a family problem," said Dad patiently.

"Well, can't you sort it out?" I asked pointedly. "You're supposed to be a counsellor, aren't you? You go to enough meetings."

He looked astonished. "Look, if I was a doctor, and I

had appendicitis, you wouldn't expect me to take my own appendix out, would you?"

I stared at him with my mouth open. "So what are you saying? That I give you a belly-ache?"

"You know perfectly well that's not what..."

"I don't believe this!" I felt furious and exasperated at the same time. "You spend your life sorting out other people's problems, so you don't have any time to sort out our problems. So when we have a problem, you have to get somebody else to sort it out. What about the person who comes round to sort out our problems? Will they be so busy sorting out our problems, they don't notice that their *own* family has got problems? And when they do notice, will they call somebody else in to sort them out?"

"There's no point in getting hysterical..."

I took a deep breath. "All I'm saying is, doesn't it make sense to try and sort things out ourselves?"

Dad looked at Mum helplessly.

"I mean, can't we just talk?" I said.

Mum said, "We do talk."

"No we don't. We don't talk because you're never here, or when you are, you..." I pointed at Mum "... are always up to your neck in schoolwork and you..." waving vaguely at Dad "... are reading notes or writing notes or preparing a case study or something. The only time you speak to me and Nick is to find out whether we want beans with our fish-fingers, or peas."

"That's not true," Mum said defensively.

But I was in full flow. Weeks of frustration and anger were being released. "You're not bothered about me or interested in anything I do. It's always everyone else. It's not fair. I hate you all!" I stormed out of the kitchen, slammed the door behind me, ran into my bedroom, put the Rock FM top forty on the stereo, turned the volume to maximum and hugged my old teddy until his stuffing came out.

There was an uneasy quiet at breakfast next morning. I wasn't going to say anything, Mum and Dad looked at each other with knowing glances and Nick just wolfed his cereal down as though nothing had happened. I left for school as soon as possible.

"That's it," she said, packing her bags. "I'm leaving you all to see the Big Wide World."

"Don't go," begged Charlie's mother.

"We need you here," pleaded her father.

Charlie picked up her bags and flung them over her shoulder along with her water-skis, snow-shoes, hiking boots, subaqua gear, crampons and ice axe. She was ready for any adventure, anywhere, anytime.

"It's no good trying to persuade me to stay. I've made up my mind. I'm off to seek my fame and fortune. Goodbye, forever!"

At registration, Amy realised that something was bothering me so we arranged a "Charlie-problem-solving-session" for dinner-time in the form room.

We met as arranged and Amy sat and listened patiently as I rattled on about the night before and life in general.

"My life is the pits! I've got a brother that I hate, parents that ignore me all the time, a part in the play that couldn't get any smaller and I fancy a boy who can't stand the sight of me. Oh Garth, Garth! - wherefore art thou Garth?"

"Actually you've got that wrong," said Amy.

"I've got what wrong?"

Amy took a deep breath. "Well, you're saying 'wherefore art thou Garth?' as in 'whereabouts are you Garth?', but when Juliet says 'wherefore art thou Romeo?', she isn't saying 'where are you Romeo?', she's actually saying 'why are you called Romeo?' because she's just found out that he's a Montague and a sworn enemy of her family, the Capulets. So what she means is, 'why does the bloke I fancy have to be a Montague?' and not 'whereabouts is Romeo?' but you're saying 'where are you Garth?' and not 'why are you called Garth?', so you've got it wrong. Got it?"

My mind was reeling. "Does it matter?" I snarled.

Amy thought for a second and shrugged. "I suppose not. Just thought you might be interested to know that what she's really saying is..."

"All right!" I shouted. "Don't tell me again. Life's too short! Honestly Amy, you think I'm so stupid sometimes and I'm not. I might only have a small bit in the play and you've got a larger part, but I'm not stupid. I was just quoting and anyway, we weren't supposed to be talking about Garth, or Juliet's lines or anything like that, we're supposed to be talking about my problems with my family!"

"Well you do go on..." Amy started to say.

"No I don't," I interrupted. "God! You sound just like my parents. Going on and on... Oh, how can you understand?" I said in exasperation. "You don't have to live with your Mum and Dad."

At that point something happened which I'd never experienced before. Amy; quiet, placid, calm Amy, exploded with rage.

"WHAT?!!!! You stupid, self-centred PIG!" she

screamed at me. "I don't 'understand'? What do you know? How would you like it if you had to live your life split between your Mum and Dad? How would *you* like having to try and get on with their new girlfriends or boyfriends all the time?"

I sat shell-shocked as Amy continued to shout at me.

"Would *you* like crying yourself to sleep every night?"

I shook my head dumbly.

"Because that's what I do. Even after all this time. You have no idea. When I'm with Dad, I want to be with Mum, and when I'm with Mum, I want to be with Dad. You've got a Mum and Dad living under the same roof and all you ever do is moan about them. You make me sick!" Amy grabbed her bag and made for the door. "I've had enough of your moaning; I've had enough of your self-pitying rubbish; I've had enough of you! "

And with that, she ran out of the form room leaving me sitting open mouthed and dumbstruck.

Amy didn't turn up for lessons that afternoon. I found out that she'd signed out of school saying she'd got a doctor's appointment. Tom asked me if I knew what was wrong with her. I told him everything that had happened. He nodded and patted me on the shoulder. "Well done Charlie," he said, sarcastically. "Ms Tactful rides again." Then he wandered off. Later on, I found out he'd signed out as well, to go to the dentist. What a coincidence, I thought sourly. My friends can't even stand being in the same school as me.

I decided that I'd ring Amy and apologise, but when I called her, she hung up without saying a word. It was the same on Saturday morning. She must have seen my number come up on her phone and she just hit "busy". Even my texts went unanswered. Some of the Nurse's lines sprang into my head:

> *O day, O day, O day! Oh hateful day!*
> *Never was seen so black a day as this.*
> *O woeful day! O woeful day!*

Shakespeare certainly knew about depression.

On Sunday I went round to Amy's. I was just about to turn into her gate when I met Tom coming out. He stopped, and blinked.

I grabbed him by the sleeve and hauled him behind the hedge. "Have you been to see Amy?" I asked.

He nodded nervously. "Yeah, well, I just thought I'd, you know..."

"I've tried phoning and texting. She won't talk to me. How is she?"

He shrugged. "She's still pretty upset."

"Do you think I should go in?"

"I don't think that would be the world's greatest idea just at the moment."

"Oh." I kicked at the moss between the paving slabs. "Well... er... d'you want to go for a burger? Or something?"

"Can't. I'm going out with the family in a bit. See you Monday."

I nodded miserably and he trotted off.

I lay in my bedroom for most of the weekend, thinking about things. I'd been foul towards my best friend, I was cheesed off with Mum and Dad and, to cap it all, it was the week of the play, which I'd only wanted to be in because I thought that I could get off with Garth.

I felt very miserable, very scared and very lonely.

ACT 4, SCENE 3

Affliction is enamoured of thy parts
And thou art wedded to calamity.

(Romeo and Juliet, III. iii)

I sat waiting for the dress rehearsal to start and feeling very uncomfortable. My costume tickled like anything and anyway, it didn't fit. Where I went in, it went out, and where I went out, it went in. All the Capulet servants were wearing the same sort of costumes, so you'd know which side they were on. They'd been run up on the sewing-machines at school, so there were threads hanging off everywhere. They were basically tubes with sleeves sewn on, stitched across the top except for a hole where your head came out. There was also a hat which Ms Hillier swore was an exact replica of what people would have worn in sixteenth-century Verona. All I can say is that people in sixteenth-century Verona must have looked like complete prats.

I had nothing to do for most of the time, and no-one to talk to. Amy was avoiding me. She hadn't spoken to me since we'd had our row. Tom was racing about backstage somewhere seeing that everybody had the props they were supposed to have (unless he was avoiding me, too, which was more than likely).

Eventually, Ms Hillier gave the cue to start, the lights in the hall dimmed, the stage lights came up and the play started. Sampson and Gregory came on. Sampson was wearing a watch; as Ms Hillier had told us all at least a dozen times to take all our watches and jewellery off, the play stopped while she nearly had a seizure. She insisted on doing the opening again.

At last the play got into its stride. Sampson and Gregory did their macho posturing bit and started a fight with a couple of Montagues. Benvolio and Tybalt joined in; Old Capulet and Old Montague arrived itching for a punch-up but their wives held them back, then the Prince showed up and laid the law down. Romeo did some whingeing to Benvolio about how The Fair Rosaline was giving him a hard time (Silly cow, I thought, doesn't know she's born). The County Paris came sniffing round the Capulets' after Juliet. Then Amy came on and played her first scene with Juliet. If you ask me, Amy carried the scene. Lady Capulet was quite good, but Deborah made Juliet about as exciting as a shop window dummy. Romeo and his pals came on and decided to gatecrash the Capulets' party and Mercutio drivelled on about Queen Mab for about twenty minutes.

Then it was the party scene where Romeo meets Juliet for the first time. I sat watching Garth and Deborah together, feeling sick and empty inside. I thought Juliet was a lot more lively in this scene; then I realised that Deborah wasn't really acting any better, she was just playing up to Garth. This didn't make me feel a whole lot happier, especially as Garth was doing everything to encourage her short of rolling over on his back to have his tummy tickled. Their kiss went on for a quite unnecessary length of time. The Nurse practically had to drag Juliet away from Romeo; for a moment, I thought Amy would have to throw a bucket of cold water over them.

After that there was the scene where Romeo hides in the garden and climbs up to Juliet's balcony. The scenery shook quite a lot at this point, but not enough to make Deborah fall off the balcony and go splat on the stage, worse luck. Romeo went and bullied poor old Friar Laurence into agreeing to marry him to Juliet in secret. Then it was time for my scene.

I stood in the wings with Amy while Romeo joshed around with Benvolio and Mercutio. Amy couldn't have given me more of the cold shoulder if she'd had it in the freezer for a week. I trudged on-stage after her, and when she asked me for her fan, she nudged me a good deal harder than she needed to, so that I said, "Ow!" instead of "Anon". I moped my way through the scene while Romeo and the Nurse made plans for the secret wedding. Then I went and sat down again.

Next was the fight scene where Tybalt stabbed Mercutio fatally in the armpit, then Romeo killed Tybalt and legged it. The Prince banished Romeo. The Nurse told Juliet her cousin was dead and she was terribly upset for about five seconds before she started slobbering over Romeo again, the heartless little madam. Romeo had a major stress with Friar Laurence, the Nurse showed up to take Romeo to Juliet and then it was the interval.

I went and got an orange juice. I wasn't thirsty but it was something to do. I saw Tom talking to Amy. He said something; she shook her head, and he gave her a quick hug. I raised my eyebrows a bit; Tom wasn't normally the huggy sort. I supposed Amy must still be feeling upset. She went backstage, and Tom spotted me. He came over and sat down.

"How's it going, then?" he asked.

"Oh, hi. You are speaking to me, then?"

He shrugged. "Why not?"

"Because I'm a selfish pig with a mouth big enough to park a car in."

"Hey, nobody's perfect."

"I never meant to upset Amy."

Tom stretched. "You never mean to upset anyone. Trouble is, not upsetting people is hard. You have to work at it."

"Don't I work at it?"

"You can't help upsetting people unless you know what they're thinking, and you can't know what other people are thinking if you spend most of your time living in your own head."

"Do I?"

"Don't you?"

I sighed. "I suppose I do."

"Well..." Tom stood up. "Better get backstage I suppose, before somebody starts playing with the swords again."

He headed for the door to the stage. Strangely, I felt a bit better. Not much, but a bit.

The second half started. Old Capulet promised Juliet to the County Paris, unaware that his dear daughter was playing Mummies and Daddies with his worst enemy upstairs at the time. Garth and Deborah had another scene in which they did a lot more canoodling than they had in rehearsal, then Juliet told Old Capulet he could tell the County Paris to take a running jump and Old Capulet went ballistic and brought the wedding forward. Friar Laurence came up with his daft scheme to drug Juliet so everyone thought she was dead (was that asking for trouble or what?).

Deborah swallowed the lethal contents of a small bottle of deadly poisonous tomato juice and collapsed gracefully on her bed.

The Nurse found her. I'd seen Amy play this scene any number of times, but it still made me cry. The Nurse comes into the bedroom bustling about, full of the joys of spring, pleased as Punch that everything's worked out all right and making rude jokes - and then she finds that Juliet is (apparently) dead, and goes off her head with grief. Amy always managed to make me feel that she really was heartbroken. This helped a lot, because my big scene came next. Well, not exactly a big scene, but the one scene in the play where Peter actually gets to do something apart from say, "Anon."

As Amy came off-stage, I went on.

"Musicians, O musicians, 'Heart's ease',
'Heart's ease' ! O, an you will have me live,
play 'Heart's ease'."

It's a nice little scene in which Peter and the Musicians who have turned up to play for Juliet's wedding desperately try to cheer each other up, but every time they try to be funny they tail off and feel more miserable than before. It wasn't much of a scene, really, but it was my special moment in the play.

After that I had nothing to do until the curtain. Romeo heard that Juliet was dead, bought some poison from an apothecary and went racing back to Verona to kill himself at Juliet's tomb, the fool. Friar Laurence found out his wonderful plan had gone pear-shaped. Romeo killed Paris, then broke through the bars to Juliet's tomb (not too difficult as they were made of plastic), swigged the poison and turned his toes up. Juliet woke up (lousy timing, eh?) and after a couple of minutes' overacting, stabbed herself to death (hooray!). The Prince swanned up and told Old Capulet and Old Montague that it served them jolly well right, and that was it apart from the bows.

After we'd scraped the make-up off and got back into our normal clothes, Ms Hillier called us together.

"I'm not going to give you notes tonight," she said, "we'll sort out any problems tomorrow before the warm up." We started reaching for coats. "Oh, just one thing," she went on. "We're still overrunning. We must get the curtain down by ten o'clock."

Huh, I thought, if Garth and Deborah cut down on some of the clinches we'd be finished half an hour earlier...

"I'm afraid we'll have to make a couple of cuts, so bring your texts tomorrow to mark them in. It's mostly a few lines here and there, but..." I closed my eyes. I knew what was coming. "One scene, we're going to have to lose altogether; the one with Peter and the musicians. It's not that you're not playing it well, it's just a time cut. Okay? Good night then, see you all tomorrow."

I sat there feeling numb. Come on, I told myself, it doesn't matter, it's only a stupid play; anyway, you have to be professional about these things, and not mind. Be professional...

But it was my scene, the only thing I had to do in this whole rotten play that I'd been working on for weeks and weeks that was really mine, and it was only a little scene, it wouldn't have hurt anybody to leave it in...

I picked up my bag and headed for the door. I thought I noticed Amy moving in my direction, but then

Tom headed her off. I didn't want to talk to anybody, anyway.

It was raining outside, which was probably just as well. I stood at the bus stop with tears rolling down my cheeks, and nobody noticed.

When I got home, Mum, Dad and Nick were sitting round the kitchen table. Mum made me a cup of tea and I sat down, trying not to sniff. Dad cleared his throat.

"Er... Charlie," he said, "we've been giving some thought to what you said the other day, and we feel that, while you need to learn to manage your anger..."

Mum coughed.

"... well, anyway, we've decided we really should give you our support, so we've decided to come to the show on Friday, and Nick has kindly agreed..."

"I didn't agree!" said Nick mutinously. "You said I had to go..."

"... *kindly agreed*," snapped Dad, "to skip bowling for once, so..."

I burst into tears and fled from the room. As I ran up the stairs, I could hear Dad complaining:

"Oh, for God's sake, now what? Honestly, there's no pleasing some people!"

ACT 5

ACT 5, SCENE 1

Spread thy close curtain, love-performing night...
(Romeo and Juliet, III. ii)

There was a knock on the dressing room door and Tom's voice shouted, "This is your half-hour call. Thirty minutes to curtain."

He was greeted by a chorus of catcalls. "Come on in, Tom!" Deborah's voice rang above the rest. "Come and see Sandra with her vest off!" Sandra squealed and threw a powder-puff at Deborah. All good clean girlie fun.

The dressing room was far too small, and packed to bursting. Each mirror reflected three or four anxious faces trying to make-up all at the same time. Girls still in school uniform jostled with those in full costume, and every stage in between. All over the place girls were panicking because they couldn't find their tights.

I had squeezed into the quietest corner I could find. Amy elbowed her way through the crush to stand beside me. She fished a mirror out of her bag and put it on the work surface in front of me. It was the shaving mirror her Dad had left behind when he went. I shuffled up to give her half a chair to sit on. She gave me a tiny half-smile and sat down beside me. She started to spread foundation over her face.

"Could you do my lashes later on?" she said after a bit. "I always blink when I have to look." I nodded. I didn't trust my voice. I'd been crying on and off all day.

"I'm sorry they cut your scene. It wasn't fair."

I gave what was supposed to be an unconcerned little

115

laugh, but it turned into something like a sob. "Ironic, isn't it? After Mum and Dad have finally worked out they can come to the last night after all, my scene gets the chop."

"My Mum's coming tonight. My Dad's coming tomorrow," said Amy quietly.

I could have kicked myself.

Tom came round to call fifteen minutes, then five. On the last call, only Deborah bothered to screech something back at him. Everybody else was probably feeling the same way I was. If there were butterflies in my tummy, they were wearing hobnail boots. I velcroed Amy into her costume. She gave my arm a little squeeze.

Finally Tom called "Beginners" and we all trooped out of the dressing room and made towards the stage.

On the notice-board in the corridor there was a card pinned open. It had a dancer on the front, posing on one leg with her arms outstretched. She was wearing a long scarf so it was probably Isadora Duncan. The message inside was: "*To Thea* (Thea? Was that Ms Hillier's first name? Poor woman!) *and the whole cast, Best of Luck for your first night.*"

Lord knows who it was from, she probably sent it to herself.

Only Deborah was feeble-minded enough to try and peek through the curtains to see who was in the audience - she shouldn't even have been on-stage - and when Tom tried to tell her not to, she gave him a very snotty look, just to remind him who was the star and who was the props assistant. Then she stalked offstage for an extra-curricular smooch with Garth. I stood there hating her. She was so mean, and so selfish...

Suddenly, realisation hit me. She was so mean and selfish? Well, what was I then?

I turned and flung my arms round Amy. "I'm sorry I was a pig and I didn't mean what I said it's just that I never thought and you're the best friend I've ever had and you're going to be the best Nurse ever and I'm sorry..." And suddenly Amy was giving me a big hug and wishing me luck and we were both crying. Then the stage lights came up, the curtains flew apart with a swish and Samson and Gregory swaggered on and started their bully-boy act. The show had started.

I stood in the wings watching the play, feeling better than I'd done for ages. Occasionally, Tom went past on some errand and gave me a grin. When she wasn't on stage, Amy came and stood beside me.

Deborah was all over Garth in the scene at the Capulets' party. I whispered to Amy, "I thought Juliet was supposed to be chaste."

Amy rolled her eyes. "If she carries on like that, she'll be chased all over the place." She sailed on stage to lever the two of them apart.

As I watched, I mouthed Juliet's lines as Deborah said them, or tried to. The trouble was, she'd never learnt her lines properly, so that she forgot several of them; and the ones she remembered were only approximately what Shakespeare wrote. In one line she said "hairy tongue" instead of "airy tongue". When she told Romeo "Yet I should kill thee with much cherishing", she had such a grip on him that it looked as if she meant it. I began to feel sorry for Ms Hillier, who was wandering round backstage, peering anxiously at Deborah and chewing her handkerchief.

Not long after that it was my scene with Amy. I stood behind the flat we were supposed to enter from, feeling sick. Amy had got over her nerves, as she'd done a couple of scenes already. She looked relaxed and cheerful. She gave me a wink and bustled on. I took a deep breath and followed, blinking in the sudden brightness of the stage lights.

Well, I didn't forget my lines or fall over anything, and five minutes later I came off again with nothing to look forward to until the curtain call.

I wandered away down to the dressing room, which was now deserted. I sat listening to the muffled voices of the actors as the play went on. It sounded like something happening hundreds of miles away, that I was listening to on the radio. I sat half-listening and let my mind wander...

"My Gahd!" Franklin Z. Mogul the Third, King of Broadway producers, bit his Havana cigar in half and tore at his greying hair. "Oh my Gahd! Three million dollars I got invested in this show, the first night crowd is breaking the doors down, the critics are baying for blood, and where's my star actress? At the Joan of Arc Hospital for Incurable Neurotics, having her goddam stomach pumped!" The Giant of the Theatre held his head in his hands and sobbed like a baby. "Ruined! I'm ruined!" He lifted his tear stained face to the desolate cast of HOOFERS IN HIGH HEELS. "Show's over, folks."

She stepped hesitantly forward. "Gee, Mr Mogul, maybe I can help; I've bin watchin' Deborah rehearse, I know all the steps..."

The producer patted her, not unkindly. "You're a sweet kid, Charlie, but..."

Suddenly, Garth Strong, the other star of the show, was at her side. "Listen to her, Mr Mogul. Sure, she's only a chorus girl, a gawky kid from outta town, but if she knows the steps... Jeez, it's gotta be worth a try!"

The ageing impressario looked up into her eager face. Hope dawned. "Hell, why not. Think you can do it, kid?" Charlie nodded dumbly. "Okay, doll. Get out there and save the show."

The whole cast cheered and raced to take their starting positions. Garth stopped Charlie, spun her round and held her in his strong arms. His eyes were moist, his dimple wrinkled. "I know you can do it, kid. I believe in you..."

"Charlie!" Ms Hillier's head was poking round the dressing room door. "Charlie! It's an emergency!"

I gaped at her. Could it be...?

"The stage manager forgot the drinks for half time! Could you nip down to the kitchen and get a couple of jugs of water for the orange squash?"

Sighing, I went.

After the bustle of the interval, I sat around until it was time to go and watch Amy's scene. She was terrific, as usual. I gave her a hug when she came off (I was crying again, but this time it was for the Nurse). After that, Amy wasn't on again, so we watched the end of the show together.

The curtains closed. The audience clapped politely. The curtains opened again and we all trooped on-stage. The minor characters stood at the back and the people with big parts came on in a sort of circus procession so the audience had to keep clapping long after they'd rather have stopped. Amy took her bow with Friar Laurence and got a good round of applause. Garth came on to squeals from the girls in the audience, looking like the cat that's broken into the dairy. His bow was barely more than a nod of the head. Deborah bowed so low I thought she was going to fall out of her dress, and got a chorus of cheers and wolf-whistles from the school football team. Ms Hillier milked as many curtain calls as she could. On the last one, most people had stopped clapping and were looking for their coats, and when the curtain opened they had to start clapping again. They looked annoyed.

Amy's Mum had been watching the show with her new boyfriend; they picked Amy up and gave Tom a lift. Amy said she was sorry there wasn't room for me in the boyfriend's flash sports car.

So I had to catch the bus alone again, but this time I didn't mind.

Act 5, Scene 2

My dreams presage some joyful news at hand.
(Romeo and Juliet, V. i)

Next day, school was pretty good.

There was a real buzz about the place. Lots of teachers were making positive comments about the show. Those that had been to the first night said how much they'd enjoyed it, those who hadn't been yet were saying how much they were looking forward to seeing it and even those who always said they'd go to plays but never went, looked as though they might change their minds.

Ms Hillier was going round with a great big grin on her face and, to be honest, so were all members of the cast - including me (despite my lack of lines). I could understand what people meant when they talked about the thrill of the stage.

After school, I nipped home and grabbed a bite to eat before heading back to school via Amy's. We changed into our costumes and nipped to the toilets for final preparations.

We found Deborah in the loos, hunched over a large black bag. She heard us and spun round like a startled rabbit.

"Oh, its only you," she said, recovering quickly. "You had me worried for a second."

"Why?" I asked.

Deborah pointed at her bag and winked in an exaggerated manner.

"What have you got there?" Amy asked.

Deborah giggled, tapped the side of her nose and beckoned Amy and me across. She opened her bag wide. There, nestled amongst her make up and spare clothes, was a large bottle of cola.

Amy and I looked at each other and shrugged. "So...?"

"Taste it," ordered Deborah, unscrewing the cap and passing the bottle to Amy.

Amy took a large swig. "Phwarrgghh!" She spat it out and began coughing for the world.

"Rum and cola," explained Deborah as Amy continued spluttering.

I was shocked. "Ms Hillier will kill you. You know she's said no alcohol backstage and definitely no drinking before the show."

"How's she going to find out?" Deborah stared threateningly at me and Amy before taking a massive swig from the bottle. "Dutch courage," she said, licking her lips. Then she headed out. Amy and I stared at each other and shook our heads.

As we wandered back to the dressing rooms, we saw Deborah in the corridor taking more swigs from the bottle and her and Garth having what seemed a minor row. Deborah was pointing at the bottle and loudly saying it was "just cola". Garth was shaking his head and wagging his finger at her. Hello, I thought, interesting...

As the time drew nearer to curtain up, Ms Hillier gathered us together and gave us a pep talk along the lines of a football manager encouraging players: "You're only as good as your next performance... You all need to concentrate... make a big effort... it may be the second night for you, but it's the first night for the audience... people out there have paid a lot of money... etc. etc. "

During her rallying call, I was trying not to laugh as Tom kept whispering behind me. "Oh yes, it's a play of two halves and five acts... We're taking it one act at a time... It's not over until the final couplet... Romeo will be over the Juliet or sick as a Paris..."

"Shush," I hissed and then began coughing as Ms Hillier caught me with one her stares.

She finished her speech with a dramatic "Break a leg everyone" and swept out leaving us to finalise all our preparations (and Deborah to take another mouthful of "just cola"). I saw Garth staring daggers at her. Hmm I thought, there could be trouble ahead. Oh good!

And then it was time.

"Beginners in place please. Curtain up in five minutes. Two minutes... To your positions... House lights down... Let's do it and make it good..."

"Break your neck, everybody!" Deborah hissed, and burst into giggles when people shushed her. The "just cola" was certainly taking effect.

Halfway through the second act, I saw Garth storming back towards the dressing room and heard him whisper, "She's plastered!" to Friar Laurence. I looked and saw that his tights had a great big ladder in. Then Amy arrived and told me that during the balcony scene, Deborah was swaying so much that she nearly fell off and then when she and Garth were embracing she refused to let go and clung to him like a limpet. Apparently Garth had to push her off, which meant that he slipped and caught his tights on the balcony.

During the interval Ms Hillier came backstage and scurried over to Deborah. "Are you sure you're all right, Deborah? You seem to be..." there was a pause as Ms Hillier sniffed the air. "You've not been drinking have you?"

"Of course not," denied Deborah as she sucked on an extra-strong mint. "Actually Miss, to be truthful, it's my time of the month. I think I'm a bit PMT-ish."

Why teachers always fall for this excuse, I just don't know, but they do (especially male teachers). Ms Hillier visibly flinched, nodded her head and said, "I understand dear. You're feeling a bit sluggish. Well, don't worry, I think you're coping very well, get through it the best you can." She half turned to go before bending down and whispering in Deborah's ear. "Try Vitamin B6 dear, it works for me."

"Thanks Miss, I will." Deborah waved ta-ta to Ms Hillier, spat out the mint and took another gulp of "just cola".

As we waited for the second-half curtain, the devil in me realised that this was too good an opportunity to miss. I wandered over to where Garth was sorting out his laddered tights and nodded towards Deborah. "She seems a bit under the weather today," I helpfully pointed out. "I just hope she doesn't forget any of her lines in your scenes. It would be so embarrassing to look really stupid in front of all those people..."

Garth didn't say anything; he just stormed over to Deborah and snatched the bottle off her.

Oh Charlie, you little stirrer I thought, as I watched Deborah and Garth having a loud "quiet word".

The second half came and went. Deborah managed to get through the play without any mishaps (shame) and we got a good round of applause (although not as good as the previous night).

When we all got back to the dressing-room, Deborah sprang straight to her bottle and began knocking it back as though it was water. Garth followed her, even though he wasn't supposed to be in our room, and tried to wrestle the bottle off her. Some of it spilt over him and he went into a major strop and marched off leaving Deborah on her own (Yeehah!). Things are going *soooo* well, I giggled to myself.

Amy and I were the last to leave - Amy had volunteered to help Tom pack up the props, so I said I'd help her. She said I needn't bother - in fact, if I didn't know she was just being kind, I'd have thought she was trying to get rid of me; but I wanted to be helpful to show I wasn't really a selfish cow. Eventually she and Tom finished putting things away and we set off for home.

As we meandered out of the school hall, we heard shouting coming from above us. We looked up and saw Deborah climbing on the metal fire escape.

"Oh Romeo Romeo, Wherefore art thou Romeho ho ho... heee heee?" Deborah burst into giggles as she swung on the railing.

"Deborah, get down," I hissed. "Someone will see you."

"Go get thee hence, for I will not away," yelled Deborah at the top of her voice. She took a final swig from the bottle and then threw it to the ground. "O churl! drunk all and left no friendly drop... With your lips I die... aggghhhhhhh!"

There was a horrendous sound of a body clanking and thudding on metal, accompanied by a series of shrieks as Deborah crashed down the fire escape then lay in a crumpled heap.

Tom, Amy and I rushed over. Deborah was squealing with pain and holding her leg. Her foot was bent at a funny angle.

At the beginning of the night Ms Hillier had told us all to "break a leg". I'm sure she hadn't meant it literally, but Deborah had taken her at her word.

Act 5, Scene 3

Ay me! What news? Why dost thou wring thy hands?
(Romeo and Juliet, III. ii)

Ms Hillier sent a note round the following morning. We were all to meet her after registration.

The stage that had glowed with warm Mediterranean colours under theatre lights looked dingy and forlorn in the morning sun. The cast of *Romeo and Juliet* sat around it looking worried. Ms Hillier stood biting her lip, waiting for late-comers. She looked as if she hadn't had much sleep.

Eventually, she said; "I phoned the hospital this morning. The doctors have told Deborah she mustn't put any weight on her ankle for at least seventy-two hours. There's no chance of her doing the show tonight. Normally, in this situation, the stage manager would go on and read the lines from the script, but I think Gail..." she looked helplessly towards Gail, the stage manager, who stood with her arms folded and a just-you-try-it look on her face... "isn't ... er...

really comfortable with that idea."

I could understand Gail's point of view. She was a terrific stage manager, very efficient and organised. Unfortunately she was also small and podgy, and as far as looks went - well, she wasn't Juliet.

"I don't want to cancel," Ms Hillier went on. "There's a full house tonight, and I don't want to disappoint people, but..." She left the sentence hanging in the air and looked at us helplessly.

I opened my mouth to speak. Then I went red and shut it again.

Ms Hillier sighed. "Well..."

"Ms Hillier!" Amy's voice broke the heavy silence. "What about Juliet's understudy?" She dug me savagely in the ribs.

"Understudy?" Ms Hillier looked bewildered.

"Charlie, Miss. She said she'd understudy Juliet weeks ago, when Deborah was off."

Ms Hillier sniffed like a duchess being offered a whelk. "Well, I mean, I don't think I actually agreed..." Clutching at straws, she said, "Do you know the lines, Charlie?"

I stood there gaping like a fish. "Better than Deborah does, Miss," supplied Amy. Under her breath she muttered, "Not that that's difficult." She elbowed me in the ribs again and hissed, "Come on, Charlie, go for it!"

Ms Hillier hesitated. "Well, I don't know."

Garth detached himself from a pillar. "I don't want to cancel tonight's show either," he said, "but the production's gone very well so far; wouldn't it be a pity..." he looked at me "... to spoil it?"

I felt anger boiling up inside me. Of all the conceited... I ignored Garth and gave Ms Hillier a hard stare. "I do know the lines, miss. And I know what Juliet does. I've been to most of the rehearsals. If you want me to have a go, I'll do my best."

Ms Hillier looked startled. "Well, I don't know," she said again.

I glared at her. She didn't think I could do it. Garth didn't think I could do it. Nobody ever thought Charlie could do anything. I felt light-headed. I turned away from Ms Hillier and stood in the centre of the stage:

> "O Romeo, Romeo! - wherefore art thou Romeo?
> Deny thy father and refuse thy name.
> Or, if thou wilt not, be but sworn my love,
> And I'll no longer be a Capulet."

There was a stunned silence. I swung round on Garth. "That was your cue, wasn't it? Would you like me to give it you again?"

Looking astonished, Garth muttered,

> "Shall I hear more, or shall I speak at this?"

I turned away from him again.

> "'Tis but thy name that is my enemy...
> What's in a name? That which we call a rose
> By any other name would smell as sweet..."

We played the scene. You could have heard a pin drop.

> "Thou knowest the mask of night is on my face,
> Else would a maiden blush bepaint my cheek

For that which thou hast heard me speak tonight."

I reached out and grabbed Garth by the lapels of his jacket. He gave a muffled squeak. I fixed him with a steely gaze:

"Dost thou love me? I know thou wilt say, 'Ay'.
And I will take thy word. Yet, if thou swearest,
Thou mayst prove false..."

Romeo and Juliet exchanged their vows of love. The Nurse called Juliet into the house.

"I come, anon - But if thou meanest not well,
I do beseech thee..."

Amy called "Madam!" again, but softly, as though she was afraid of breaking some spell.

The lovers arranged to meet at Friar Laurence's cell. The scene came to its close. It was time for Romeo and Juliet to kiss. Garth looked for a moment as if he might try to stop me, but he couldn't have done it with a shotgun. I kissed him; not like Deborah, and not like Charlie; but as Juliet saying, "You are mine..."

"Good night, good night! Parting is such sweet sorrow
That I shall say goodnight till it be morrow."

I turned away from Garth, moved upstage, and stood still.

Nobody sniggered.

Somebody started to clap.

Then suddenly, everybody was clapping and whooping with delight. It was relief, really. I looked up into Amy's eyes. She was clapping harder than anyone, and giving me a brilliant smile.

I turned to Garth. He still looked wary, but he nodded. I gave a weak smile in return. I'd try for admiration, but I'd settle for grudging respect.

Ms Hillier became businesslike. "Well, it looks as if we might have a show after all. Right, we'll need Capulet, Lady Capulet, the Nurse, Friar Laurence and Paris for rehearsals... and you, Garth, of course. Let Gail know what classes you'll be missing and I'll send a note round. We'll rehearse Charlie into the party scene with everyone else at six, the rest of you come back then." As the stage cleared, she turned back to me.

"Well now... we'd better get to work."

Act 5, Scene 4

Oh, blessèd, blessèd night! I am afeard,
Being in night, all this is but a dream...
(Romeo and Juliet, II. ii)

I stood in the wings, having kittens.

I jumped a mile when somebody tapped me on the shoulder. It was Ms Hillier.

"Charlie, would you like me to make an announcement before the curtain?" I looked at her blankly. "You know, actress playing Juliet indisposed... how you pluckily stepped in at the last minute, that sort of thing...?" I shuddered and shook my head. "It's just that... in case the audience might need to... make allowances..."

I glared at her and shook my head. "They won't have to. Anyway, if you tell them, they'll just sit there squirming in their seats waiting for me to do something wrong."

Ms Hillier stared miserably at her shredded handkerchief. "Well, perhaps you're right..."

"They've all got programmes, haven't they?" Ms Hillier's first year drama class had spent their lesson time sitting at the back of the theatre stuffing programmes with little notes giving the cast change, while Ms Hillier rehearsed me into Juliet's scenes. One of the first years was Nick. He'd whispered something to his mate and they'd both sniggered. Then Amy had had a word with them both, and there hadn't been any more sniggering.

Ms Hillier nodded unhappily and wandered off, while I stood rigid with shock. I'd just realised: Nick would be in the audience tonight - and so would...

I turned to Amy in panic. "Mum and Dad! They're coming tonight..."

Amy made shushing noises. "Don't worry. They'll be fine. You'll be fine."

I stared at her. "What am I doing here? How did I get into this? I'm just about to go out in front of two hundred people, including my own parents, in my nightie... I must be mad!"

Amy gave me a shake. "Get a grip, soldier." She gave me one of her famous grins. "You're going to be terrific."

"I'm going to be sick."

The stage lights came up, the curtain opened. The show began its final performance.

From the start, it was clear from backstage that it wasn't going well. People were nervous. Samson and Gregory fluffed their lines in the opening scene. Somebody's sword broke in the fight scene and somebody else caught a blade across the knuckles. Garth took three prompts in Romeo's scene with Benvolio. Then they went off, and Lady Capulet came on:

"Nurse, where's my daughter? Call her forth to me."

Amy turned towards the wing where I was standing:

"Nay, by my maidenhead at twelve year old,
I bade her come. What, lamb! What, ladybird! -
God forbid! Where's this girl? What, Juliet!"

That was my cue. I stood rooted to the spot. I couldn't have moved to save my life. I'd lost my bottle. I could hear the audience getting restless.

Amy, acting her socks off, shrugged to Lady Capulet, said, *"What, Juliet!"* again, came off stage and dragged me on behind her.

It was my line. Somebody had tied a knot in my tongue. I couldn't remember my first line. I couldn't remember *any* of my lines. How could I ever have imagined I could stand on a stage in front of hundreds of people and remember what I was supposed to say? My face began to burn. If Deborah's tan made her look like an authentic Italian, my blush was making me look like an authentic tomato.

Amy improvised a line:

"Now, Juliet; your mother calls."

As she said this, she moved round so that her back was to the audience and pulled a funny face. She crossed her eyes and dangled her tongue out of her mouth, showing me how gormless I looked, just standing there.

It worked. I turned to Lady Capulet.

"Madam, I am here. What is your will?"

Practically fainting with relief, Lady Capulet picked up the next line. Then Amy started on the long speech where she goes on and on about the silly joke her husband made when Juliet was a child... and suddenly I was laughing. Not acting, but really laughing, because Amy was so funny... and after that it was all right.

The party scene started. I danced with the County Paris, and then I came face to face with Romeo.

"If I profane with my unworthiest hand
This holy shrine, the gentle sin is this..."

Suddenly I was back in our sitting-room at home, reading the lines with Garth before Nick's stupid spider had spoiled everything. Not this time, I thought.

"Good pilgrim, you do wrong your hand too much..."

I played the scene with Garth, teasing him, laughing at him. When he kissed me, and Amy came and separated us, I blew him a mischievous kiss as I went. Not because Ms Hillier had directed me to do it, because it's what Juliet would do.

The balcony scene sailed by. The audience stopped rustling. People stopped dropping lines. The performance started to flow.

In the midst of all this, a horrible thought struck me. Who was playing Peter?

I looked round, and realised that Tom wasn't wearing the normal stage management black; he was dressed in Peter's costume, which was several sizes too small for him. He gave me a shamefaced grin. I gave him a grin back, and whispered in his ear, "If in doubt, just say 'Anon.' You'll be right two times out of three."

Everything went swimmingly until we reached the scene where Juliet meets Romeo at Friar Laurence's cell to get married. What was supposed to happen was that Romeo and Juliet go into a clinch on Friar Laurence's last speech and hold it until the curtain is drawn. Well, I was kissing Garth (and enjoying it) when I realised that Friar Laurence had finished talking, and the curtain still hadn't closed. I shot a glance off-stage to see Tom (still in Peter's costume) wrestling with the cord. The curtain had jammed.

With my lips tightly pressed against Garth's, I said, "Wock goo we goo now?"

With his lips tightly pressed to mine, he said, "I goank know."

I could see panic rising in his eyes, so I said, "Shall we geck off?"

"How goo we goo gack?"

"We cug shuckle off sigeways..."

"Gno!"

Oh well, I thought, snuggling closer as Tom tugged frantically at the cord off-stage; waste not, want not...

Benvolio said to me in the interval, "Those love scenes you do with Garth... phew!" He ran a finger round the inside of his collar and grinned. "Hot stuff!"

The lights came up on Juliet's window. Romeo stood beside it, lacing his jacket. As I took a breath to say my first line, I remembered that this was the last scene I had to play with Garth; and after it was finished, and the play was over, he'd probably never look at me again. So there was a quaver in my voice as I stepped behind him and said,

"Wilt thou be gone? It is not yet near day..."

As Garth turned to face me, I realised something else. He was acting with me. He wasn't just saying the lines in a showy way, as he'd done with Deborah; he was living the scene. He was involved.

"O, thinkest thou we shall ever meet again?"

Garth took my hand, and kissed my palm, and Ms Hillier never directed that, either. Romeo said:

"I doubt it not; and all these woes shall serve
For sweet discourses in our times to come.
Dry sorrow drinks our blood. Adieu, adieu!"

And then he was gone.
Well, it was nice while it lasted.

It's very difficult to lie completely still for ten minutes, but that's what Juliet has to do while Romeo fights Paris and then goes on for ages about death and how Juliet shall have worms for her chambermaids (cheerful stuff, eh?) before he swigs the poison and pegs out. Then I had a nasty moment when I realised Garth had gone and died lying on his dagger, so I couldn't stab myself with it. I had to roll him over, which I don't think was in the script (and I'm certain that Romeo shouldn't say "Ow!" after he's dead, but he said it quietly so I don't think anyone noticed). Then I had to stab myself and lie there dead (pretending to be really dead this time, not just pretend dead) for another five minutes while Friar Laurence tried to make out the whole thing wasn't really his fault (well, whose was it then?). And then it was the end.

I don't think there was more applause than there had been on any other night, but there wasn't any less either. And it would be nice to say that as I took my bows, I thought of Deborah, and felt sorry that she wasn't there to share the moment with the rest of us...

But I didn't.

Act 5, Scene 5

I dreamt a dream tonight.
(Romeo and Juliet, I. Iv)

For the next few minutes everything was a blur. I remember Ms Hillier meeting us all off the stage and trilling "Well done! Well done!" and her saying to me "Very impressive, Charlie! Well done indeed! I never knew you had it in you." I think all the cast slapped me on the back (it certainly felt like it) and I'm sure that there was loads of whooping and laughing and lots of cries of "It's all over!"

I drifted back into the dressing-room where there was a large bouquet of flowers for me and a card that said "We're all very proud of you. Love Mum, Dad and Nick" and, although I'm pretty certain that Nick wouldn't have agreed with those sentiments in a million years, it made me cry and Amy gave me a hug.

Then Garth put his head round the door, called me over and said "Incredible. I just don't know how you did it," and I just shrugged and went to jelly. Then he said. "Look forward to seeing you at the party," and he winked and I must have beaten the world record for not breathing. Maybe Romeo and Juliet hadn't played their last scene together after all...

When everyone had changed, we all helped clear props and costumes away while Ms Hillier set up a trestle table in the middle of the stage. She'd brought some fizzy Italian plonk, some cheesy nibbles and paper plates, and when everything was cleared away it was time for the speech.

The rumour was that she'd given the same speech for fifteen years. Ms Hillier started by saying that she wasn't going to go on for very long (and we all cheered, even though we didn't believe her). She said lots of nice things about everyone and how it was the best cast she'd ever worked with and I got a special 'the show must go on' mention.

Someone shouted out "What's the next play going to be?" and Ms Hillier laughed and said, "I think I need to get over this one first!" Then we all gave her three cheers and Amy presented her with a bouquet that all the cast had chipped in for (it wasn't as big as mine!) and then everyone dived into the food and Italian fizz.

I stood back looking out at the empty seats taking it all in. When I turned round HE was standing at the back of the stage, staring at me and smiling and I felt myself staring and smiling back. Then we began to move towards each other. At last! After all the heartache, all the hours of dreaming and all the longing, Garth Strong, Most Desired Male and Sex on Legs, First Class was mine. YESSSSS!!!!!

Charlie stood with Garth on the deserted beach. Waves crashed on the shoreline and palm trees were silhouetted against the bright vivid orange fireball that was the setting sun.

Garth held Charlie's hand tightly. "I love you," he declared. "With all my body, with all my soul, I love you..."

"It's Deborah! She's here!"

Everyone turned to the stage door.

Deborah was in a wheelchair. She looked pale. Her face was set with determination, but betrayed the pain she was bravely suffering, just so she could be with us all. She turned melting eyes on Garth, and reached out a trembling hand, as if to say, "I am so sorry, can you ever forgive me?" Her eyes shone with unshed tears.

It was easily the finest performance she had ever given.

There was a sudden rush as people crowded around her to ask her how she was and give commiserations. I looked on, horrified. There, standing in the midst of the throng, was Garth. Next to her. Right next to her. Staring. Into her eyes. I heard Deborah mumble something like, "Sorry Garth, I was a fool," and then he knelt down and was hugging and kissing her and there was a cheer and I ran off the stage and out into the corridor as quickly as I could.

In the toilets I splashed water on my face. I was shaking with rage. I looked long and hard in the mirror and saw a total idiot! How on earth could I have ever fancied Garth I'm-So-Shallow Strong? Why had I put myself through all that torture? I mean, he'd seen Deborah. He'd seen for himself how stupid and selfish she was, and he still...

And he'd seen me. All those hours pining after him, telling myself that if he'd only look at me for once, if he'd only see the real me, he'd understand how I felt about him and then.... But tonight, he had seen the real me. He'd seen me do something that Deborah could never do if she lived to be a hundred, and he'd acted Romeo with me as if he meant it, and yet the minute Deborah turned up he was all over her like a rash, and I was completely forgotten...

I'd read about the 'scales falling from people's eyes' and wondered what it meant. Now I knew.

Garth was a lightweight. He was an airhead. Okay, he'd got good looks, wasn't a bad kisser (not that I had enough experience to make comparisons) but underneath he was... *a loser*!

If I actually thought about the way Garth played Romeo, I had to admit that he wasn't really as good as I'd thought he was (and nowhere near as good as he thought he was). He'd said some lines as if he didn't understand them, and he only did any acting when he had lines to say; when he didn't, he just stood around and waited for his next cue. Mr Self-obsessed or what? I never wanted to see Garth Strong again.

I splashed more water on my face. I felt as if my brain was taking a ride on a rollercoaster.

Why did I want a boyfriend anyway? Probably because lots of other girls had them, so they must be okay; and I didn't want to be left out. But were they worth the trouble? A boyfriend shouldn't make you miserable; a boyfriend should be a laugh, someone you got on with, who made you feel good and...

For the second time since I dived into the loo, I felt as if I'd had an electric shock.

"Stupid! Stupid! Stupid!" I shouted at the mirror. Who was the one boy who thought about me, who LIKED me, who made me laugh, who looked out for me? TOM! Tom, who I'd known since juniors. Tom, who was my best friend (after Amy). He'd even tried to ask me out at half-term, and I'd been so stuck on Garth I'd barely even noticed. Tom!

And he was back there at the party, waiting...

Charlie stood with Tom on the deserted beach. Waves crashed on the shoreline and palm trees were silhouetted against the bright vivid orange fireball that was the setting sun.

Tom held Charlie's hand tightly. "I love you," he declared. "With all my body, with all my soul, I love you."

She held him tightly. "I love you too, my darling."

As the waves crashed onto the shore, Charlie swore that she could she hear violins playing.

Tom knelt down on one knee and took her hand in his. "Will you be mine forever?" he asked...

Back in the hall, there was still a crowd around Deborah and Garth was still attached to her like a limpet but I didn't give them a second thought. I was looking for Tom. Would he even look at me after the way I'd treated him? I'd been a fool, but he knew that anyway. Perhaps I could just go up to him sort of casually, and...

And then I saw him. At the side of the stage next

to the curtains. With Amy. Kissing her. And she was kissing him back. Big time. I stood blinking and unbelieving. My second best mate was getting it on with my best mate.

When they came up for air, Amy saw me gawping and winked at me. I gave a sickly groan and winked back. Amy mouthed "Better than kissing your grandad," and I grinned and turned away feeling sick and betrayed, although I had no reason to.

What did I expect? I'd practically driven them together. I thought back to all the things I'd have noticed if I hadn't been mooning over Garth. Tom's visit to the 'dentist'; Tom round at Amy's house; giving her a hug; the lift home in the sports car; Amy waiting for Tom and helping him put the props away, and me insisting on being helpful even when they'd rather I...

I gave a hollow groan. I wasn't only an idiot, I was a gooseberry.

I wandered over to the trestle table in a daze and picked up a bottle of the fizz. Empty! I wanted to cry but I felt drained and all out of tears.

"Er, Charlie, isn't it?"

I turned round. There was a boy standing next to me. A tall boy.

A tall, blond, blue-eyed, boy. With a nice smile, and a gentle voice.

And he was talking to me!

"Y.. y.. yes," I stammered.

" Hi. I'm James Prince. I'm from the City Sixth-form College. I'm writing a review of the play for the local paper and I wanted to ask you a few questions. Do you mind?"

I shook my head and he led me over to a chair and sat me down.

He smiled the biggest, brightest smile ever. "I wanted to say that I thought you were amazing. Incredible. For me you *were* Juliet. Passionate, sensitive, perfect for the role..."

My mind was reeling as he continued to lavish praise upon praise.

Charlie stood with James on the deserted beach. Waves crashed on the shoreline and palm trees were silhouetted against the bright vivid orange fireball that was the setting sun.

James held Charlie's hand tightly. "I love you," he declared. "With all my body, with all my soul, I love you."

She held him tightly. "I love you too, my darling."

As the waves crashed onto the shore, Charlie swore that she could she hear violins playing.

James knelt down on one knee and took her hand in his. "Will you be mine forever?" he asked.

She didn't hesitate. Pulling him up towards her she cried. "Yes, James. Yes, James. Yes, yes, yes!"

Their lips met in a passionate kiss ...

A long while later they turned and walked together hand in hand into the sunset and their glorious future.

Well, a girl's got to dream...

The Epilogue

A bit of peace at last, this morning brings.
   Our tale is done, there's no more to be said.
More cruel than the wasp's are love's sharp stings;
   Oft, those who suffer wish that they were dead.
And here, alas, we end our tale of woe;
   Will Charlie ever find her Romeo?